TROOPER #4

Published by Mundania Press
Also by Noah Chinn

Bleeding Heart Yard

TROOPER #4

NOAH CHINN

A Mundania Press Production
Mundania Press LLC
6457 Glenway Avenue, #109
Cincinnati, Ohio 45211-5222

To order additional copies of this book, contact:
books@mundania.com
www.mundania.com

Cover Art © 2012 by Wyatt Chinn
Edited by Holly D. Atkinson

Trade Paperback ISBN: 978-1-60659-341-7
eBook ISBN: 978-1-60659-340-0

First Edition • July 2012

Production by Mundania Press LLC
Printed in the United States of America

10   9   8   7   6   5   4   3   2   1

To Hanna, Felice, and Gillian

One and the Same

The vast courtyard within the castle walls exploded with life. Commoner and noble alike were awed by the fountains of sparks that shot from brass barrels high into the evening sky. Tantalizing smells both sweet and savory drifted on the wind, along with music and laughter.

A young girl of three years wandered alone through the festival, her eyes filled with curiosity. She looked at every man and woman as if each was the most amazing thing she'd ever seen. Older children played with a ball in a clearing, but she wasn't interested in their games. The simple pleasures of an empty apple crate were more enthralling. It could be a cart, or a fort, or a boat...

Musicians, singers and actors warmed up for the evening's performance. Nearby, people waited patiently in line to gaze at the growing number of stars through the Royal Astrologer's wondrous spyglass. And next to them a bard sang the history of the land—great battles fought, great deeds done.

The girl was alone, but wasn't afraid. It wasn't in her nature to fear such a wonderland.

෴

She ran. Through forests, streams, and hills the girl ran till she could run no more. There was no thought behind this, only instinct and timing.

The city was dead. Lia was dead. *Everyone* was dead. Everyone but her.

Exhausted, she collapsed at the top of a wooded hill. For a moment, she thought she saw a man hunched over a campfire, a strange blue dome next to him. But it was just her imagination. There was no man here—only trees, dead leaves, and darkness.

Shivering, the child covered herself in leaves and slept.

DAY 1

The day started like any other. The sun came up, and in twelve or so hours it would go back down again. The world could end and this would still be true.

The early light of dawn filtered through brown curtains, staining the walls of the small bedroom. A woman in white briefs and a T-shirt slept on top of the brown covers, her arms and legs sprawled across the double bed like the chalk outline of a homicide victim.

The light began to drill through her eyelids. She winced and turned her head, but her brain had already started waking up. She opened her eyes. Beside her was a brown chair, a blue shirt and dark pants crumpled on the seat. A belt draped over its back.

Her brow furrowed as she tried to make sense of what she saw. The clothes seemed out of place, like a pimp at a funeral. Were they hers?

She lifted her head to scan the room. There was no sense of familiarity, none of the comfort you felt when you woke up at home.

Her heart beat faster; she *wasn't* home.

It began to race when she had to admit she didn't know where home was.

She sat up, grasping at the details of the room. A large TV sat on the dresser across from the bed. Beige carpet covered the floor. The bathroom door stood wide-open—white tiles and porcelain dimly lit by a small pane of frosted glass. No one there. The front door was shut, a notice framed on it. She got up for a closer look. No words, just a diagram of the room.

She opened the curtains and let the light pour in. Outside was a parking lot connected to a two-lane road with a police car stopped on its shoulder. Beyond that was nothing but dry grassland. Next to the parking lot was a tall sign—MOTEL—with an arrow that arced over the word and pointed down.

She went back to dress and stubbed her toe on something hard. She winced and looked at her feet.

A long pump shotgun lay on the floor next to the chair.

She jumped back as if the weapon would shoot her of its own free will. It must have fallen over, having been propped against the chair. For a moment, her fear came from recognition; part of her *knew* why the gun was there. As soon as she felt an answer creep forward, her mind pushed it back into the shadows. She looked to the nightstand. Next to the lamp was a black automatic pistol. She looked at the clothes on the chair again and saw a metal star glint on the blue shirt.

It was a uniform. The nametag under the five-pointed star read: T. Felice.

She had no idea if that was her name.

She tried on the clothes, put on the belt, but didn't touch the guns. The uniform fit, but the nametag in the mirror was as indecipherable backwards as it had been forward.

She was a cop? It didn't seem to click with her. Aside from the guns and uniform, she could have been a reporter or an aristocrat and it would have made as much sense.

She looked back to the pistol on the nightstand. It was a Glock 22, which held fifteen .40 caliber rounds and was standard issue for many U.S. law enforcement agencies. The shotgun was a Mossberg 590. She was pretty sure not many rich aristocrats knew that. Maybe if they lived in Texas.

She looked at the nametag again.

T. Felice.

Tonya? Tiffany? Tammy?

These names belonged to someone with a trust fund.

Toni? Thelma? Tash?

Those didn't feel right, either, but Felice sounded okay. Felice it was until further notice.

She picked up the remote off the dresser and sat on the bed. She turned on the TV. Nothing. She pressed the power button again, tried to turn on the power manually, unplugged the set and tried another socket. Nothing.

Felice tried the lamp next to the TV, then the one on the nightstand, then the main room switch. No power anywhere. Great.

There was a jingling in her pocket. She fished out a brass key attached to a plastic tag twice its size. On one side, it said *MOTEL*. On the other, *104*.

Felice went to the door. She turned the handle, and then changed her mind. She went back, picked up the Glock, put it in the holster, and propped the shotgun back against the chair.

The air was still brisk this early in the morning. She walked out into the parking lot, which was empty. There was no sign of anyone else at the motel. There was no one in the police car across the road. It was most likely hers, too.

She raised her hand to her eyes and scanned the horizon, but there was little to see aside from flat grassland. Distant mountains skirted the edge of the world, and though the sky above was clear, dark thundering clouds loomed beyond the range.

Five or ten miles past the motel sign, a small city stuck out of the grassland like a concrete island. But it was all wrong. Smoke rose from half the city in thick black plumbs, and once or twice she saw a lick of flame. Barely visible at this distance on the road was a pile up of cars that spilled off the shoulder and onto the grass. They, too, were smoking.

The day had started like any other. The sun came up, and in twelve or so hours it would go back down again. The world could end and this would still be true.

It had.

Felice ran back to the motel. Her instinct was to grab the shotgun, but by the time she was inside she realized how pointless that was. There wasn't another living soul in sight. Apart from the city, the pile of cars, and the mountains in the far distance, the motel was the only thing around. *She* was the only thing around.

Agoraphobia hit hard. She felt like a speck of dust in the grassy void of existence. She closed the door and braced herself against it, panting. For a moment, she thought she'd never leave the room again.

Felice shook her head. Whatever was going on, hiding under the bed wouldn't help. She went back to the mirror. She didn't know how amnesia worked, but knew different kinds were brought on by different events, such as injury or trauma. She didn't see any bumps or bruises on her head, but judging by the burning remains of civilization down the road, trauma was a pretty safe bet.

She'd hoped the person staring at her in the mirror would have some answers. She didn't. Short black hair, deep blue eyes, a shape somewhere in that healthy range between fat as a cow and thin as a bean pole (Were those farm metaphors? Was she raised on a farm?). Her reflection didn't look familiar, but didn't look unfamiliar, either. She could have looked like anyone and she might have had this same numb non-reaction. A man's reflection would have surprised her, though. That was something.

"This is me," she said to the mirror. "Whoever I am."

She stepped back outside, a sudden wave of claustrophobia beating out her agoraphobia. On the assumption it was morning, she had some basic compass bearings to work with, but there was just as little to see out here now as five minutes before. A fresh billow of smoke and fire appeared on the far end of the city to the north and drifted upward, but that was all.

She strode to the police car. At least she could do something productive. The cruiser was a dark blue—so dark it was almost black—with two yellow stripes and the state police star on the doors. The passenger's side door was jammed shut with a deep dent; dust covered the hood and lights. She got into the driver's seat and tried to start the engine. Dead. Not even a whine.

"Goddammit."

She popped the trunk but found only a spare tire, jumper cables, and an empty gas can.

Felice looked back at the hotel. Not another car around? She could understand a place like this being empty, but what about the owners? Surely they lived here and had a car. Though if the city was any indication, maybe they were smart and got the hell out of wherever-she-was.

Where *was* she?

A hundred yards in either direction was a sign on opposite sides of the road, both facing away. She walked to the sign farthest from the city.

NOW ENTERING
FORT ROCK CITY LIMITS
POPULATION 4000

The city was visible between the sign's legs. Four thousand? One of the zeros must have fallen off; the city looked bigger than that. Presumably the sign closer to the city had a standard NOW LEAVING CITY LIMITS on it, perhaps with a rustic PLEASE COME AGAIN tacked underneath. She covered her eyes from the sun to scan the rest of the world. Still nothing, aside from the dark clouds behind the mountains.

So I am T. Felice of the—she checked her star—*Oregon State Police. I'm at a motel at the edge of Fort Rock. I have no memory, my car is dead, the city is on fire, and I slept with a pistol and shotgun within easy reach last night. Other than that, it looks like a nice day.*

It was true; aside from those behind the mountains, there wasn't a cloud in the sky.

Felice sighed. There was only one place to go that didn't require several hours hike. It couldn't hurt to make sure the motel owners weren't home. Maybe this lot was visitor parking only and their cars were somewhere behind the building. It was worth a shot.

The single storey motel was built in an L shape with a dozen rooms along its length. The short, disconnected stub at the bottom would be where the manager lived. A small restaurant or convenience store sat beside it, or perhaps they just offered a jug of OJ and plate of donuts as their continental breakfast. At the very least, there were a couple of vending machines outside.

At the door to the manager's office her gaze caught on something: the door was ajar (which was promising) because the lock had been forced (which was not). The splintered wood on the doorframe made her uneasy.

Felice looked down at her right hand. She had drawn her Glock without realizing it.

With her left hand, she slowly pushed the lobby door open, listening for anything out of the ordinary. Weapon ready, she stepped inside. Empty. She moved, slow and silent, behind the wood counter and checked every corner, but found nothing aside from a water cooler. She looked at the keys on the wall behind the counter. Only Room 104 was missing.

She holstered the gun and began to relax. The break-in had probably been her own doing. She'd arrest herself later.

God knew what was going on in Fort Rock, but for now, at least, she was okay. She had to believe that or she'd snap. Given her amnesia she'd most likely snapped once already. She tapped the desk bell, which shattered the suffocating silence, then just as quickly faded.

"Hello? Anyone there?" She didn't expect an answer and wasn't disappointed. Felice checked the phone. It didn't work, of course. The motel register was open on the counter, but she couldn't make out the names—they were just so many chicken scratches. Cheating couples and hookers with their johns trying to avoid a paper trail. The last name on the list wasn't hers, but then she hadn't seriously believed she would break into a motel fully armed, steal the keys, then politely sign the guestbook.

She rectified that now, taking a pen and writing *T. Felice* on the first fresh line, then *104* under the room column.

She looked at her handwriting. Very neat, not something you'd expect from someone who could kick in a door. She wrote in the comments box: *Clean and tidy. Wasn't disturbed all night. Would recommend to all my friends, if I knew who they were.*

Felice searched the rest of the building. The manager's room was locked. She found a key under the counter. No point in breaking down every door in the place.

It was another motel room, much like her own. The designer couldn't have won many awards for creativity. The bed was made. The window didn't face the sun, so the room was dim and filled with shadows. Felice shut the door.

As fear subsided, long term planning began to take root. She had to check the power, try to get the car running, and try to contact, well, *anyone*. She also had to hunt for food, and the restaurant was right next to the reception area. She wasn't hungry—not yet—but it was the easiest thing to take off her list.

The restaurant was well lit by three full wall windows. It was more of an enclosed patio than a solid structure. The blinds were up so she could see the main road. The smoking remains of the city were clear in the distance, as was the stalled cruiser about a hundred yards behind.

"Don't mind me, I'll find a spot." Felice sat at one of the white hardtop tables, food forgotten for now, and watched the smoke and fire.

"What the hell happened?"

The scenario she had pieced together was this: she had bolted from the city like a bat out of hell, only to stall outside this motel. When she couldn't locate a manager, she'd broken in, taken a key, let herself into a room, undressed, and collapsed in exhaustion.

Whatever happened in Fort Rock was bad enough she *really* wanted to forget.

She sat there, trying to make sense of the hell on the horizon. Another plumb of fire and smoke rose from a building. It would have been massive if seen up close, but from the restaurant looked like a tiny puff of orange and black.

"One Mississippi. Two Mississippi. Three Mississippi. Four..." She stopped counting after twenty, then, a few seconds later, heard a dull rumble. The fact there wasn't so much as a breeze to hinder the sound unnerved her.

How did that work again? Five seconds to the mile? Five miles away? Maybe she was counting fast. Felice snorted. It was a pointless question. How about a better one: what was on the menu? Pancakes. She definitely felt like pancakes. And eggs. And bacon. And sausage. But mostly pancakes.

Only...if there was no power, anything in the fridge had probably spoiled; even if it hadn't, what would she cook with?

Felice looked to the kitchen and got up. *Maybe they have Froot Loops.*

From the corner of her eye, she saw movement on the road. It caught her attention because it was something, not the same old nothing that existed along the rest of its length, surrounded by more grassy nothing.

Someone was walking out there. Felice strained her eyes to make out who it was.

Who cares? It's someone!

She abandoned the hunt for dry breakfast cereal, ran out the door, and took to the road. People meant cooperation, support, and answers.

It turned out long stretches of nothing could skew your sense of depth perception. At first she thought the person was maybe a mile down the road. Turned out he was a lot closer, and a lot shorter.

She slowed down as she reached him. He couldn't have been more than nine or ten. He shuffled forward—dressed in a blue private school uniform—but didn't react at all to Felice. She knelt before him; he almost bumped into her, but stopped at the last second.

"Hey, you all right?" she asked. The boy didn't respond. Something told Felice to back up. She did, and the boy started moving once more. He swayed slightly from side to side, then stopped again when he reached her. Felice had the strange feeling the kid was moments from lunging and eating her brains. She looked at his downturned face. His skin was pink and healthy; his eyes looked normal.

"Are you all right?" she asked again. Still no response. "My name is Felice. I'm a police officer. I want to help you, okay?" The boy still stared at the ground, as though patiently waiting for her to get out of the way. When she did, he continued to shuffle forward. Felice followed alongside him.

"Can you talk?" Apparently not. "Are you hurt?" Apparently not. "Can you tell me what happened?" Apparently not. "Geez, give me something to work with, here, kid." She was starting to get angry. "Tell me about yourself."

The boy stopped and blinked. Her words were starting to sink in. Sometimes you need to kick with a boot instead of brush with a feather. She tried to keep the momentum going. "Where are you from?"

The boy turned and pointed to the burning city. "Gone."

"Pretty much figured that one out, thanks," Felice muttered under her breath, then repeated her earlier question. "What happened?"

The boy looked at her. His eyes were of the kind of hazel you couldn't quite pin down, and his hair was somewhere between light and dark brown. He had the most confused look on his sad face.

His mouth opened and closed a couple of times, as if searching for words that wouldn't come.

"Hey, you're okay now. I'm going to take you somewhere safe. Follow me, okay?"

The boy didn't nod, but followed. It would have been faster to carry him, but that didn't feel like the right thing to do, like he might throw a tantrum or have a seizure if she tried. Instead, she stayed a couple of steps ahead and kept to his pace. All this time having walked away from a burning city, alone...he had to be in shock, and unbelievably tired.

Despite the school uniform, he couldn't have been at school today. This scale of destruction didn't start and end in the span of a couple of hours, and most of the fires had burnt themselves out. The boy must have hidden overnight and wandered this way at daybreak. If he was dressed for school, whatever happened in town probably occurred between 8am and 4pm yesterday—perhaps the day before.

She looked at Fort Rock again. Assuming it (whatever *it* was) happened yesterday, and since this wasn't Old London Town, the fires couldn't have simply spread from building to building. They must have started in a whole bunch of places.

A stranger and more immediate question was, why the hell was one of said burning buildings moving toward her?

Felice's eyes widened. It wasn't a building, but a truck. She picked up the boy and ran off the road. She saw people burning on the hood and roof of the car, and heard a scream as it roared past in flames, but even that couldn't quite cancel out a deep, empty droning noise that chilled her to her bones. The truck suddenly veered off the road and slammed into the motel restaurant as if guided by a homing beacon. The back end of the truck exploded.

"Oh hell no." Still carrying the boy, Felice ran back to the motel, to Room 104, and set the boy down on the bed. "Stay here!"

Felice grabbed the fire extinguisher and axe from the manager's office. The smell of burning flesh, gas and rubber filled her nostrils, making her stomach twist. She couldn't put the truck out with one lousy extinguisher, but hoped to keep the fire from spreading. Fortunately, the office and restaurant weren't directly connected to the other rooms.

She chopped and dragged what flaming bits of the structure she could and blasted others with the extinguisher until the canister went dry. Hours passed before she felt comfortable leaving the blaze alone, though she made time to check on the boy every so often. Eventually, the fire seemed to give up and burn itself out, leaving the restaurant gutted and the manager's office singed. The wrecked truck and the bodies both in and on the vehicle sat in the center of the restaurant like some morbid college prank.

Blackened from soot with a number of ember burns on her clothes and hands, Felice wiped the sweat from her forehead, making a flat grey streak. She checked her watch. It was stuck at 11:02. Great. That didn't work, either. She gave a deep sigh. It didn't matter what time it was. The rest of the madness could wait until tomorrow for all she cared.

Felice went back to her room, exhausted. The boy was asleep in his clothes. She couldn't blame him. He lay stiff on his back, not curled up or on his side. If his hands had been crossed over his chest, he'd have looked like a funeral display.

She went to the bathroom to wash up but stopped at the door. She didn't want to go inside. Something at the back of her mind screamed at the thought. Her hand drifted toward her gun as she peered in. There was more light now that the sun was starting to drop behind the motel, and what came in bounced off the white porcelain and tiles so she could see everything.

It was empty, but not unused. The shower curtain had been torn down, bits still stuck to the rod's metal rings. The rest was left on the floor. Something could have been hidden underneath. Felice went back for her shotgun, then used it to drag the plastic sheet aside. Nothing. So why had she torn it down? What had she been afraid of?

A sudden need to use the toilet overrode her concerns. For all she knew, she'd been holding it in for a week. The instant she flushed she regretted it—no hiss came from the tank, just a gloosh down the bowl. She confirmed her fears by checking the taps at the sink. No fresh water.

"Of course there isn't." Felice looked at her hands and didn't even want to look in the mirror. She'd probably scare the kid back into a coma when he saw her.

They wouldn't get very far without water, that was for sure. Felice went back to the manager's office. There had been a water cooler by the reception desk that she could drag back easily enough. There were also the vending machines outside. One was big and red with a generic COLA logo running down its side. The buttons offered such famous brand names as Cola, Orange, Lemon-Lime, Root Beer, and Water. The other machine was full of junk food; chips, cookies, gum, and candy of a variety a remote place like this could afford.

She had no change. Not that it mattered, because there was no power. Not that it mattered, because she had an axe.

Soon the room was filled with all the junk food and soda a kid could wish for. She spent some time arranging the treasure on the long dresser, building soda can pyramids and laying out the other goodies like piles of gold and silver. Maybe it would cheer the boy up when he finished his nap. Thinking along more practical lines, she set up the cooler in the bathroom and kept the bottled water in the top shelf of the closet. She didn't want to waste those.

Now she took the time to wash herself. She didn't feel like bothering with a full sponge bath, though, just enough to get the grime off her exposed bits. Her hands were speckled red from the embers, but her face was fine, more or less. Just sooty.

Before she went back outside, she checked on the sleeping boy again. His chest barely moved but otherwise he seemed okay. At this point she was just trying to stay active. Find something to do. Be productive.

She went back to the police car and popped the hood. Perhaps the problem was just a loose wire or something. Maybe she could start it up again.

It turned out she couldn't even be sure which part was the engine.

"I guess I never studied mechanics."

She left the hood up as a universal roadside symbol for S.O.S. and sat in the driver's seat. She checked the glove compartment. A pair of high-powered binoculars nearly fell out. She hung them around her neck.

The smoke at the restaurant had almost completely died, the destruction inside was clearly visible. She went back to inspect it. All was quiet now, other than the occasional crack of the broken glass she stepped on, or metallic crinkle from the wreck cooling. The gas tank had blown outward, destroying only the back half of the truck.

Whoever had been on the roof had been thrown off, and laid in a crumpled heap in the corner. The charred remains of the one on the hood were fused into place. One of its arms had gone right through the now-melted windshield, and even now reached out for the driver. The driver had tried to get out, but had gotten stuck and died with his head out the open window, jaw wide open in a silent scream.

Felice's eyes were drawn back to the body on the hood. Most of the meat had burned away, but something was wrong with what she was seeing. She came for a closer look and bumped into the body's jutting leg, which broke at the ankle and crumbled to dust.

Felice jumped back. It was as if the body had been cremated in the fire, yet somehow held together. Bodies didn't do that, did they? Felice still felt herself drawn to the corpse. Something else was wrong. The skull. What was wrong with the skull? The eyes. Or, more accurately, where the eyes had been.

She backed out of the restaurant rubble. What was wrong? The world had gone to hell, that was what was wrong. The only sign of civilization in any direction was on fire, that was what was wrong. The only other survivor she'd come across was sleeping like a corpse and was probably more fucked up than she was, that was what was wrong. Three people had almost run her over in a rolling ball of flame and all she could think about was there was something odd about their eyes, *that* was what was wrong. The only thing that was right was she was alive, and she couldn't even be a hundred percent sure about that.

Time had slipped by faster than she expected. The sun had dipped under the dark clouds hanging by the westward mountains. There wouldn't be much useable daylight left. Felice went back to the room.

My room. I might was well stake a claim. Or perhaps our *room since I'm not about to make my little guest get his own. But since he's not here "my room" would still be correct*—"Why the hell am I thinking like this?"

The boy still slept like the nearly-dead, and Felice didn't feel that far behind. She locked the door, then secured all other possible entrances.

Satisfied, she checked the shotgun and placed it under the bed within easy reach, then put her Glock on the nightstand. She tried to relax. Then she got up and made sure there wasn't a round loaded in either weapon before lying down again. Accidents happen.

Her mind searched for answers to explain the insanity that had passed. She found nothing, other than the typical end-of-the-world thoughts one would expect.

End of the world. Maybe something here had the answers after all.

She opened the nightstand drawer and sure enough, there was a Gideon bible inside.

She flipped to the back for The Book of Revelation, and landed on Chapter 6.

> And I saw when the Lamb opened one of the seals, and I heard, as it were the noise of thunder, one of the four beasts saying, Come and see.
>
> And I saw, and behold a white horse: and he that sat on him had a bow; and a crown was given unto him: and he went forth conquering, and to conquer.

Felice rolled her eyes. *That clears things right up. Thanks.* What did she expect to find, anyway? People brought up Revelations because it was *about* the end-of-the-world, not because it had detailed instructions on how to survive it. The last thing she needed was a lesson in eschatology.

She turned the book to the beginning. She wanted to see the start of life, not the end. Unfortunately, the introduction and first page of Genesis had been torn out. The book started at Chapter 3. She must have had a religious upbringing, because she knew what that chapter was.

"Straight to the Fall of Man." She considered skipping to Exodus. That had the flight from Egypt and plagues and the death of the first born son and all that jazz. At least it felt relevant.

It was getting dark and she found her eyes straining. What she saw on the page didn't make sense and she didn't feel like reading bone-dry scripture, anyway. She put the book back in the drawer, then stared at the ceiling, wishing she could remember happier times.

She was in a lush forest. Trees grew thick and tall like castle towers, and were alive with the sounds of birds and other animals. Ahead lay Görlitzhafen, city of commerce and learning. Its population had swelled in recent years, attracting merchants and thinkers alike from across the realm both for the trade of goods and ideas.

The curtain wall surrounding Görlitzhafen had been expanded twice over to accommodate this growth; while the city itself was peaceful, the world it belonged to was not.

She followed the cobblestone road, laid ages ago but kept in fine condition, right up to the massive gates. The first time she tried to enter she'd been turned away. She bore no invitation, but refused to let that stop her—it had been too long since she'd seen such an event! She had to get inside, no matter what.

She'd given it some thought, and had disguised herself as a humble servant. She was able to lose herself in a crowd of similarly clad women, carrying food and wine over the drawbridge. This time the guards gave her little more than a passing glance.

Once inside she dropped the long drab shawl, revealing the far more fetching outfit she'd worn underneath. The festival was about to begin and she wished to be dressed appropriately. People had come far and wide to attend; great knights and noble lords, whose deeds were told by the troubadours of every nation would be *here* and she would see them. She overheard someone say that even the king's court magician was attending. It had been so long since she'd felt such excitement.

The city was filled with life, the clucking of chickens in their coops, people calling out their wares or services, children playing, fire roasted meat and ale sold as fast as it could be ordered. The crowd carouselled around her with banners and bells and smell of hand spun candy. She felt like singing, but decided against it. No point in drawing attention to herself so soon.

For a woman who hadn't left home in ages, this was all she had imagined it to be and more. She wanted to see it all, talk to everyone, experience *everything*...

DAY 2

Felice stirred to the sound of a roaring fire. For a moment she thought she was attending a festival of some sort. As she crept toward consciousness, she realized roaring fires in motel rooms were *bad*, especially when one slept in close proximity to them, and woke with a start. She fell off the bed, still in her dirty uniform. A can of soda rolled off the nightstand and landed on her forehead.

"Ow!"

There was daylight, but not much. She got up and found the boy in front of the TV, eating a bag of chips as loud as humanly possible. He hadn't seen Felice fall or the can land on her head; he hadn't even reacted to the sound. Instead he ate chips and watched the blank screen.

She got up with a groan. "Really? I fall on my ass and you don't even giggle? That would have killed in Peoria, kid." Wherever Peoria was.

The boy continued to look at the TV, as if he expected it to turn itself on and entertain him. Felice didn't know what to do. Weren't some kind of magical maternal instincts supposed to kick in about now? Shouldn't she be going all Mary Poppins or something? She opened the curtains and surveyed the outside world.

Police car with its hood up on the shoulder of the road? Check.

Hacked open vending machines? Check.

Restaurant reduced to a pile of charcoal with a truck inside? Check.

Smoldering city of death and destruction in the distance? Check-a-roony.

Felice realized she was doing *it* again. God knows how many people had died in the last two days and she was using words like *check-a-roony*. Was that normal? Did she do it before she lost her mind? Did she do it *because* she lost her mind?

She sat on the bed to put on her low-cut boots, and noticed the nice polished leather had been covered with burns, scratches, and gouges while putting out the fire. Not that it mattered; it wasn't like she would be in a parade any time soon.

She took the binoculars to check on the car and the motel area, which she'd already begun to think of as her 'patrol.' She looked back at the boy, still watching a blank screen, still eating chips.

"Sit. *Staaaay*. Good boy." Not even a twitch on his lip.

She went to the car and tried starting it again—as if that would work—and then searched the vehicle from top to bottom for anything that might be useful. She found a flashlight stuck under the seat, but that was all. She turned it on. Nothing. Great. At least it could be used as a club. She slung it through a loop on her belt.

She checked what was left of the restaurant for embers. She accidentally stepped on the hand of the body that had been flung off the truck. Just like the foot the other day, it crumpled to ash and dust, as if it had barely held together this long.

The body on the hood still chilled Felice. The eye sockets were just *wrong*. They weren't empty and neutral, they had a pained expression. Eye sockets didn't have expressions. By contrast, the body of the driver looked normal—for a blackened skeleton with the flesh charred to its bone, that is. It made the tormented face on the hood, forever reaching out for him, that much more terrifying.

She pulled her gaze away and looked toward Fort Rock. It seemed most of the fires were out. There were a couple of fresh pillars of smoke, but that was all. From this distance, it was hard to make out specific damage.

She used the high-powered binoculars to get a better look, bracing them against what was left of a support beam for stability. The tall office buildings in the center were each blackened all the way up on one side. The smaller buildings had their fair share of damage, but some seemed untouched. That was good. She even saw a tiny glint of light that could only have come from a neon sign. That was also good. Someone still had power.

Today she'd have to do something more pro-active. The junk food and bottled water wouldn't last forever. She was going to have to scout out the city.

She looked back at the motel and wondered about the boy. She couldn't just leave him there.

"Oh great, *now* the hormones kick in."

It was a tough choice, but if she brought him along he'd slow her down and make things that much harder if there was any trouble left in the city. She promised herself she'd be back well before sundown. Still, she had to let him know where she was going first, even if it didn't register with him.

Felice went back to their room and knocked on the door frame to get his attention. "Hey, sport. I'm going to have to go out for a while, but I'll be back before the sun goes down, okay?" The boy watched her, but didn't react. It was like he didn't understand a word she said.

She went the caveman route. "Me leave. Go town. Bring back good food. No junk." She gesticulated with broad motions. He stared at her. "Me Tarzan. You Jane?" Still nothing.

Felice slumped down on the chair by the dresser, crinkling an empty potato chip bag. This was hopeless. "Just tell me your name. Please."

The boy blinked. Then blinked again. "Richie."

Felice sat up. *It speaks!*

"Timmy," he corrected.

"Hey, you don't have to make up a name. I'm a friend. What's your real name?"

"Mikey."

"Why did you call yourself Richie and Timmy?"

The boy shrugged and looked at the ground. "Dunno."

Well, it was progress. At least he was engaging her. She could live with it if he'd made it up; she didn't know her first name, either. Maybe they had the same kind of amnesia.

What were the odds of that?

"Okay, Mikey. I'm Felice," she said. Mikey said nothing. She hammed it up with a sloppy Jersey accent. "Wha, dey don' teach youse etiquette in dat fancy private school of yours? Between drinking tea wiff your pinky out and knowing which is the salad fork an' all, don' dey teach youse to say 'nice to meet youse'?"

"Nice to meet youse," Mikey said dutifully.

"That's better." She dropped the voice and studied the boy. He wasn't scared to talk. He didn't seem unresponsive so much as blank. She looked into his eyes. No, not completely blank. There was a spark of *something*. The eyes weren't fixed forward into empty space, they moved left and right—especially once she stared at him too long.

"Listen, Mikey. I have to go for a while, but I'll be back before it gets dark, okay?"

Mikey shook his head, so slight she almost missed it, like someone screaming "No!" a mile off.

"You'll be fine. Don't open the door for anyone unless they say the magic word. You know what the magic word is?"

Another slight shake of the head.

"Mister Bumblebum. You know who Mister Bumblebum is, right?"

Shake.

"Mister Bumblebum is a great big bear from way up in the mountains, over there. Bigger than any bear you've ever seen and then some. He likes most people, especially children, but he really *hates* mean people. Scares them off whenever he sees them. Last I heard, he was seen around these parts. So if any mean people come around here, you can bet he'll get to them first. So we'll use that as our password, okay?"

"Okay."

She wondered where that had come from, or why she'd bothered. Maybe she thought it would help bring him out of his shell. Maybe it did. She almost caught a crack of a smile on his face. But she didn't know where the name had come from, or why she made him a friendly bear. Perhaps it was part of her own locked away past. An imaginary friend? The name of her childhood teddy? A character from a picture book? An actual giant friendly bear that scared away mean people? Okay, the last one seemed pretty unlikely.

Felice mussed up Mikey's hair, and when he didn't take any action to fix it, did it for him. "You'll be fine. I won't be too long." She looked at the blank TV screen. "Find something to read. That crap will rot your brain."

She looped the binoculars around her neck, grabbed a bottle of water and fit some cookies into her pockets. She took the shotgun in one hand and made sure the door locked behind her. From the parking lot, she looked to what was left of Fort Rock and took a deep breath.

This would be one hell of a hike.

Felice figured she was walking three miles an hour at the most, but without a watch, she could only guess how long she'd been traveling. She was less than halfway to the city and already could tell it was farther than the five miles she'd estimated. She had an easier time gauging her progress through a small outcropping of rock a few miles to the west, which provided parallax between her and the mountain range.

She passed the time trying to amuse herself. She looked for the ways her situation was exactly the opposite of something out of a fairy tale, say Hansel and Gretel. The adult leaving rather than the children. Heading toward civilization instead of getting farther away. She wasn't leaving bread crumbs behind, and even if she did, there were no birds to eat them. She didn't need breadcrumbs anyway; how do you get lost on a straight road in an open plain? There was no gingerbread house and no witch with an oven waiting for her. She hoped.

Next up, how her situation was nothing at all like The Three Bears. For one thing there was the distinct lack of porridge around...

The problem with distance and perception was its exponential nature. Every hour Fort Rock seemed just as far as it had the hour before. One mile was as good as ten under an unrelenting sun.

Then all at once she was close, very close, and on top of the city.

A pile up of burnt cars and trucks blocked the road ahead. It spilled out well past the shoulders, creating a dam of twisted steel, glass, and rubber. Felice cradled the shotgun. She knew what would be next. The bodies. Eventually, she'd have to come across them. But all evidence suggested she was a cop; she was probably trained for this.

The flaming truck from yesterday must have gotten around this mess somehow. And what about Mikey? Had he been in one of these cars? Felice shook her head, trying to ignore the smell of charred meat and gasoline. It wasn't important.

It turned out there weren't as many bodies as expected. The cars piled at the front were so burnt out the passengers must have been cremated. Ash littered the road, and with no breeze, simply coated the asphalt and grass like gray snow.

The cars toward the back were also empty, though she saw a few bodies slumped inside against the wheel or dashboard. More often than not, the doors were open. They must have fled back to the city; there was simply nowhere else to go.

The first building she clearly made out was a strip joint. It was hard to miss, given the sign was a woman on her back, one leg straight up and the other angled. Several smashed-up big rigs told her this had been a trucker hangout. The building itself was badly damaged, but she doubted she would find much there except alcohol and glitter anyway. She didn't have time to sift through every building; it had taken hours to get this far, and she still had to get back.

Now that she was in the city, the destruction took on a new terrifying unreality. The central buildings, rising fifteen stories or more, looked like marshmallows that had gotten too close to God's campfire. The largest had been so badly gutted she could see sky behind it.

Beyond the strip club, the city officially began. There was basic housing here, mostly destroyed by fire. The yards, however, were untouched and still green. They looked completely out of place given the arid climate, and with no one to water them, they'd soon turn brown under this sun. On one lawn was a girl's pink bicycle, and across the street lay a red wagon on its side.

Farther down the street were stores. That was hopeful. Most of the businesses had smashed windows, many had been ravaged by fire, but one was more or less intact. The same one she'd seen with her binoculars; a small neon OPEN sign flickered red and blue.

She scanned the area for movement and walked down the center of the road toward the building. It was a camping store, solid concrete painted in green and black, but no name. She knew it was a camping store because of the logo decals on the window: trees, mountains, and a deer head. The end of the world comes and the only place not wiped out sells survival gear. Go figure. But she wouldn't argue with fate when there was looting to be done.

The door was locked and the windows were barred from the inside. The glass was webbed in one corner but intact. Fragments of green and brown bottles littered the ground underneath. Scorch marks covered the brick at the bottom. The window panes seemed tempered—bulletproof, perhaps—which helped explain how the store hadn't been destroyed.

"Ooooh, *that* kind of survival store..."

This begged the question of whether anyone was still inside. And if they still had power, maybe they still had water. Hell, they might have enough food and weapons to outfit an army. Felice could bring Mikey here tomorrow; it looked as good a fort as any under the circumstances.

She looked at the burnt office buildings at the heart of the city. On second thought, this might be too close to Ground Zero for her liking. She tried the door again, as if it wouldn't be locked *this* time. The OPEN sign flickered behind the fractured window, mocking her. There was a rustle. The Venetian blinds behind the iron bars snapped apart a couple of inches. Two gray eyes stared at Felice, then narrowed. The blinds snapped back.

Felice pounded on the door. "Open up! Police!"

The reinforced green door had a metal eye slot, which shot open. A long black barrel slid out, forcing Felice back a good two feet. A gruff voice, bordering on caricature, said, "Ask me if I care."

Felice stood her ground. "Put the gun away. I'm with the Oregon State Police."

"How's that workin out for ya?"

Felice saw his point. Her badge didn't really mean much anymore. "Sir, I'm not here to hurt anyone. I just need your help."

"Ain't no sirs here. An' ain't no help I kin give you. Yur one of the damned, jes like the rest. Ain't no one kin help you. You best git gone before them screaming mimis hear you."

"Please. There's a little boy waiting for me. I found him out on the road and I'm the only person around who can help him."

"What's his name?"

"Mikey."

"Dat his real name?"

"What does that matter?"

"'Cause I says so."

"He says that's his name."

"Can't help him."

"What is wrong with you?"

"Nothin. Aim ta keep it that way."

"Fine. You're all barricaded in there, you'll probably withstand anything short of a nuclear bomb. I don't know how many people you turn away a day, but I have to ask—"

The barrel wobbled as Felice heard the distinctive *chu-chack* of a shell being loaded. It was a universally understood sound, the kind that said, 'get off my lawn.' Or, in this person's case, *git.*

"Be careful what you ask, missy."

"Can—you—spare—any—water—food—or—equipment—please?"

The barrel wavered, then disappeared behind the slot, which shut with a clang. Felice wanted to kick the door and tell him to go to hell. Instead, she turned and walked off. There were probably a few other buildings she could scavenge. There was still time.

She reached the road when a bell rang. She looked back in time to see the green metal door slam shut. On the ground was a very large red knapsack, stuffed to the gills. Felice ran back and hoisted it onto her shoulders. "Thank you!"

The slot slid open. "Quiet, ya idjit! I don' want any unwelcome visitors."

"Then why do you have your Open sign on?"

There was a sputter from behind the door, as if the old man had accidentally spat out his dentures.

"*Godangit!*"

The blinds rustled as a small hand scrambled and felt around the window, until it found the pull cord to the sign. He yanked it so hard it snapped off. The eyes returned to the slot.

"Now git goin'. And if you run into anyone like you, don' tell them where you got that from. Understand?"

She looked at the almost featureless green and black building. "How can I? Your store doesn't even have a name."

"You think dat's an accident?" The slot slapped shut.

The backpack weighed at least fifty pounds. She didn't bother to check its contents, but a small tent and sleeping bag were bungeed underneath. She gauged the time from the sun. Good enough for today. Time to head back.

As Felice reached the pile-up that marked the boundary of the city proper, she heard someone call from behind. She turned. It wasn't the crazy survivalist, at least, she didn't think so. She didn't imagine that particular person would wear a suit. She saw him waving his arms, running toward her, but stopped when he noticed her shotgun. The man's dark gray jacket was open, his striped tie looked as if he'd tried to take it off but gave up halfway through. His glasses were askew; one of the arms had broken. He resembled a stockbroker escaping Mad Max's vision of Wall Street.

At first, the man looked afraid, then wary. Then a smile came over his face and he started running toward her again. Did he recognize her? No, he was probably relieved. Aside from being the only other person around, she was uniformed and armed. That had to seem like some kind of safety. The man looked more and more excited as he approached, as if salvation was upon him and Felice was its harbinger. She doubted she could live up to the hype.

From one of the burnt houses, another figure emerged and ran straight for the stockbroker. It looked like a man, but moved like a wild animal on two feet. By the time Felice registered what was happening, she didn't have time to raise her shotgun, let alone call out a warning. The creature tackled the survivor to the ground.

Felice ran to pull the attacker off him. She cursed the weight on her back, but it would have taken longer to drop the knapsack. The stockbroker was pinned at the shoulders; she heard the man's muffled scream; the thing on top of him only made a low unrelenting moan. It looked as if their heads were fused together, but that was impossible. They were too close to one another to risk a shot, even with the pistol. Felice swung the shotgun like a club and knocked the moaning creature off, breaking the seal between their faces. The stockbroker gasped and scrambled away. The attacker rolled onto its back, then looked at her.

The face now staring at Felice was woven from the fabric of nightmares.

The man, if you could call it that, had no eyes, only wide deep voids that fell into forever. The corners of the voids seemed to be pulled down, like its face was putty manhandled by a suicidal artist. The mouth was a toothless scowl of anguish and hunger. Even as she took this in, the creature moaned and scrambled back to its feet. Felice leveled the shotgun and fired into its chest. The sound deafened her as the blast knocked the thing back onto the ground. It didn't get up.

She turned her attention to the survivor, who was still gasping a few feet away.

"Thank you," he said. "Oh thank God. Not me. Please not me."

Felice helped him up. "You're all right now. Come on." She looked to see if more of these horrors were around. "I'm Felice. What's your name?"

The man slowed his breathing and was about to answer, then his jaw dropped. "I...I don't know. Oh God...*I don't know.*"

An unkind part of her thought he was acting like a sissy. "It's okay. I don't really know my name; I just got it off this tag here. I have a kid back at the motel down the road, and I'm pretty sure he doesn't know his either. We're going to start a club, make some t-shirts, invent a secret handshake...you like decoder rings?"

The man who looked like a stockbroker shook his head. His gaze darted around as if looking for anything familiar. "No. No, you don't understand. I *knew*. I knew who I was. Just a minute ago, I knew who I was. *I know I knew!*" He fell to his knees. "No...not after all this." He began to blubber and gave a wet sniffle.

The unkind part of Felice wanted to call him something worse than a sissy, though it still ended in –ssy. She had to keep him focused, give him a purpose. "Listen, more of those things might be coming. If they are, I'll have to hold them off. If we get separated or if something happens to me, you keep going down this road until you see a motel. There's a kid in room 104. Tell him 'Mister Bumblebum' and he'll let you in. If something happens to me, *you must take care of him*. You got that? He's counting on you."

The man nodded. He stared at the ground but began breathing easier. Truth was she wouldn't trust this guy with a bag full of sponges, but she had to give him something to hang onto, and Mikey was all she had. At least the thought of this wet blanket being the boy's last hope was a great motivator to stay alive.

"Now tell me everything you remember. Tell me what happened."

The eyes of a drowning man looked up at Felice, willing to take any lifeline, but not knowing where to grab. "I remember the voice. *Her* voice. That's the first thing I remember." He seemed to struggle to find the right words, and got more and more frustrated when only simple ones came out. "She asked a question, and everyone *knew*. And then we were afraid. I ran. We all ran. But some were already like him." He pointed to the motionless body. Felice refused to look directly at it. It might look back. "I was in an...office? Tower? Building. And I hid there. I hid there until he came. A day? He came and helped us get out. He protected us from them. Lots of them. He had to go. He said find haven. He pointed. He was in a...truck? Jeep? Car. And he was gone."

"Who is 'he'?"

The man's face looked strained. "I don't know. I don't. Dark hair. Tall. He left. We didn't agree where to go. We went different ways. Ones in groups were taken, I saw. I found a place to hide. I was alone, but I knew who I was, and I felt more alone. I don't know where to go. I heard you, and I ran to find you, and I found you."

The whole of his memories had been expressed as a mish-mash of half-coherent sentences. The unkind part of Felice suddenly felt like a jackass.

"You're all right now. You're just suffering from shock. You come back with me and we'll take care of you. Okay?"

The man nodded. "Yes. Thank you."

Felice smiled. She was becoming a regular Florence Nightingale. At this rate, the motel would be full of desperate amnesiacs and she could charge rent.

"So, how do you like Gordon for a name?"

The man looked unsure. "Gordon?"

Felice shrugged. "You look like a Gordon."

Gordon nodded. "Okay."

"Right. Let's go."

They started south on the road that would take them back to the motel. All in all, Felice felt pretty good about today.

"Don't worry, Gordon. You'll love our place. Just had the bedroom done. Mind you the kitchen needs a lot of work."

"Who's Gordon?"

Felice looked back. "You are, dumbass..." Her smile faded. Gordon's eyes began to sink, then fell into an endless abyss inside his own head. The void widened and pulled at the corners. His cheeks sunk and his lips drooped, as if at the last moment he had realized what was happening. He fell sideways onto the pavement.

Felice backed away and raised the shotgun, waiting for Gordon to get up. He didn't. All was silent except for a faint rattling noise. She looked down and saw the shotgun shaking in her hands. She looked back at the man's anguished expression.

She turned and threw up on the lawn of a burnt house. The knapsack felt ten times heavier as the blood abandoned her muscles. There hadn't been much inside her other than cookies and chips. She fell to her hands and knees, staring down at regurgitated junk food.

She had to get out of here. She looked up and saw the pink bicycle lying on the lawn, and remembered the red wagon across the street.

In another time and place, the thought of a police officer riding a pink bicycle with a red wagon in tow down the highway would have amused Felice, but right now there wasn't anything amusing about anything. She couldn't even bother ringing the oversized handlebar bell as she reached the motel parking lot. The world had gone to hell, and she didn't even know which one.

The situation was so far removed from reality the only way she could even try to relate to it was through myth. As near as she could tell, this wasn't the Apocalypse or Ragnarok; there was a distinct lack of warring deities in the area. She hadn't seen Kalki riding a horse, there were no floods, and no giant serpents hungrily eyed the sun.

She approached the problem from a different angle, based on what she *had* seen. That thing she shot wasn't a zombie. Not really. There was a certain superficial comparison, but that that was it. The scenario didn't fit any kind of virus she could imagine. What else was there? Bottom line, she didn't know what it was. If she didn't know that, what chance was there of surviving?

None, that's what.

Consider—if you lived during a plague outbreak in the Middle Ages, you were screwed. You had no idea where Death was waiting to ambush you. You'd try all kinds of crazy useless amulets or wards, or kill cats and witches by the cartload because you had no one else to blame.

But imagine the edge you'd have if you figured out the fleas on rats carried the Black Death. You learn the rules, you have a shot. Simple as that.

Felice had to find the flea. Maybe she just had to flee. She wasn't sure yet.

She fished out the key to Room 104, then stopped. Had Mikey come any further out of his shell?

"Mister Bumblebum," she said aloud. "Will you let me in?" She pressed her ear to the door, but heard nothing. Felice frowned.

Just as she put the key in the lock the door opened. Mikey stood at the entrance, looking at her. He didn't smile, but for the first time since finding him, the lights looked as if they were on upstairs. His eyes were alive, engaged. Given what had happened in town, it was the most beautiful thing she had ever seen—amnesia be damned. "I told you I'd be back, right?"

Mikey nodded. Felice left the bike and wagon outside, but dropped the knapsack on the bed.

"It's Christmas in July, and I have Santa's bag. Let's see what St. Nick brought us." Felice sniffed the air. Something smelled bad. Smelled like...

She looked around the room. About a quarter of the junk food had been eaten. She had been gone all day. It had to have gone somewhere. Like the bathroom, with its toilet that had no running water and had used up its single flush...

"Oh no." She had taken care of business by a shrub on the way back, and discovered one of the many items on the red backpack was a collapsible shovel that doubled as an axe. Mikey had eaten more than her, and, well, kids are kids so...

She went to the bathroom. The lid was down, the toilet almost looked apologetic for what it would reveal. She pulled up the lid and lurched back. It was worse than she thought. The junk food hadn't sat well with him. Felice couldn't justify wasting the water needed for a flush—several flushes in all likelihood. With some toilet paper, she disposed of what she could outside, burying it with the shovel, then sacrificed a can of soda to rinse out the bowl and give her hands a lemon-lime scent. A splash of water on her skin got rid of the sugar coating, but there was no point in wasting the whole bottle. She made a mental note that the other toilets should still have full tanks in case they ran out of the bottled stuff.

"Okay, kid, new rule. This is the Old West, the bathroom is outside, and this is your toilet-maker." She held up the now-dirty shovel. "Got it?" Mikey nodded. "Good."

With that unpleasantness taken care of, Felice went back to unloading the knapsack. Inside there were several dried or vacuum-sealed packs of food along with a couple dozen power bars. Enough to keep them going for a couple weeks. There was rope, thread, fishing line, first aid, candles, a butane lighter, a hand cranked radio and flashlight, a compass, whistle, flare gun with a box of twelve flares, and other useful odds and ends.

She gave the whistle to Mikey. "Keep this with you at all times, okay? That way you can call me for help if Mister Bumblebum isn't around."

She set aside a few candles. It would be good to have some light after the sun went down. She tried the flashlight. No power, but it wasn't charged. She tossed it to Mikey, who sat on the floor. "Here's a really fun game for you. Wind this till your arm falls off." She chuckled as Mikey dutifully began turning the crank. Tom Sawyer would have loved this kid. Every fence in town would get a double coat of paint.

Now that she had time to relax, her mind switched to more important things.

The flea.

Other than the bible, the nightstand drawer contained motel stationary: a letter sized pad and a fifty-cent pen to go with it. She pulled them out and began to jot down what she had learned.

What had the stockbroker said? 'Her voice.'

Felice jotted down: *Who is She?*

'She asked a question, and we had to answer.'

What question?

'I hid there until he came...He protected us from them.'

Who is He? Tall, brown hair. Just another survivor? Does He know more?

'I knew who I was.'

Felice's pen hovered over the page. She had no idea what to do with this.

I know I knew.

Memory seemed to be a connecting theme here. Why? Had she and Mikey been taken by one of those things? She began sketching the face she'd seen. If they had been attacked, why weren't they dead and hollow like Gordon? No, that couldn't be it. She looked at what she drew, almost all the detail was on the hollow drooping eyes. It occurred to her that she'd seen those eyes before—on the hood of the burnt out truck.

She wrote down: *They take your memories and leave you like them.*

Why?

HOW?

She underlined this several times.

"How's the winding going, Mikey? Arm tired yet?" Mikey nodded and handed the flashlight/radio to her. She turned it on. The beam started off bright but quickly dimmed. Probably needed more juice. What about the radio—what did the rest of the world have to say about this mess? Did they even know? Maybe this madness was confined to Fort Rock and nobody could spread the word.

Felice felt she was being watched, and she was right. Mikey was staring at her. His expression was less blank by the minute. What was that look? Expectation?

"Good job."

She swore Mikey smiled, but that might have been a trick of the light, or lack thereof. The boy sat back down. She heard chip bags crinkle. Without thinking she said, "No more junk food, it will give you nightmares," which amused her for all kinds of reasons. First off, any nightmare she could imagine had to be better than reality. But it was a *motherly* thing to say, and up till now she'd been treating the boy as if he came with an instruction manual written in Korean.

The crinkling continued. Felice put the flashlight/radio down and moved to the front of the bed. She was about to tell him to put the chips away again, then realized the bags were empty. He wore one on each hand like mittens. He moved the corners of the bags with his fingers, first on one hand, then the other.

To an adult this might look like nonsense, but Felice understood instantly. Puppets. Granted they had no heads, but in Mikey's mind they were puppets. Somehow, on the motherly scale, this sign of mental activity ranked up there with baby's first steps. She lay down at the foot of the bed, resting her head on her folded arms.

"Whatcha doin?" she asked.

Mikey didn't respond, wrapped up in his own little play. She could faintly make out some of the words.

"I can't believe they can afford a balloon," said the Salt and Vinegar bag.

"Got it on sale," said the Sour Cream and Onion in a deeper voice.

"This is annoying," said Salt and Vinegar.

"We should have taken a different route," muttered Sour Cream and Onion.

The story made no sense, but she had come in during the middle.

Then Mikey began to scream. "Back the fucking truck up! Get back! Shit!" Both chip bags were in a frenzy. Felice couldn't tell who was supposed to be saying what, but it didn't matter; the panic on Mikey's face was real. She pulled off the bags and grabbed his arms. He struggled and screamed something about "getting her out!"

"Mikey! Calm down! Look at me! Look—At—Me." The boy obeyed. The struggling slowed, then stopped. "It's okay. You're okay."

She wished she could believe that. Her heart lodged in her throat; she was afraid, at any moment, Mikey's eyes would sink into his head. That man had forgotten everything even while he had been talking. How could you fight that?

Felice looked at the chip bags. He'd been re-enacting something. "Is that what happened to you?"

A pause, then Mikey shook his head. Felice frowned. Either he was lying or he didn't want to talk about it. She tried a different tact.

"Talk to me, Mikey. Tell me about yourself. Where did you grow up? Do you remember?"

Mikey looked out the motel window. "In the city."

"You mean Fort Rock?" Mikey nodded. "Do you remember your mom and dad?"

A shrug and nod.

"What were their names?"

"Mom and dad."

"What were their real names?"

Mikey's face strained. "Don't want to."

"You have to. It's important."

"No!"

Felice pressed the interrogation, her tone friendly but firm. "Do you have any pets? Can you swim? What's your favorite color? What's the name of the school you go to? Do you have any friends? What games do you like to play?" Mikey covered up his ears and began rocking back and forth, but she had to get him thinking about himself, keep him remembering, even if he didn't respond.

But what if the stockbroker hadn't died because he forgot, but because he tried too hard to remember? What if *that* was the flea? She had no way of knowing.

She hugged Mikey to stop him from rocking. "Okay, okay, no more questions. I'm sorry."

Maybe for now, ignorance was bliss.

She picked up the flashlight/radio. "Maybe we can find a radio station somewhere. Do you like musi—never mind, forget I asked." She turned it on and got static, but it died almost instantly. "You're kidding." These were supposed to give ten minutes of power for every one minute spent cranking, and Mikey had wound it for at least five.

Well, he was just a kid.

She wound it again and turned it on. There was the static hiss of dead AM air, which faded in seconds. It wouldn't hold a charge. "Stupid fricking defective machine." She wondered if all the food the hermit had given them had expired, too. Fortunately, she could keep the radio powered like an organ grinder.

Using her thumb to tune the radio while she cranked, she searched for a working station, but found only different flavors of static. Then the pitch jumped; she'd found something but overshot it. She slowly worked her way back.

"...and two more Moaners walking down Fifth." The voice belonged to a young man, definitely not the survivalist hermit. "That's about all for now. The sun's going down, and as much as I'd like to keep talking, me and Yuri can't risk giving away our location by turning on the lights. The Moaners might not listen to AM radio, but we all know they can see even if they don't have eyes." There was a pause, and a faint hiss of static. "Maybe I'm just talking into the void, people, but I can't—I won't believe that God has forsaken every last one of us. If you believe in Him, and believe He has a plan, then that plan has to include the rest of us pulling together and helping one another. It has to. Otherwise, what's the point? I'm doing my part. Now ask yourself, what are you doing?"

Felice looked to Mikey, who was on his knees, his head resting on the bed, watching her wind the radio.

I'm doing plenty.

"I'll be back on the air shortly after sunrise. That's a promise. As always, we're monitoring the FM, AM and Ham radio bands for anyone else out there. If you can broadcast, try using the following channels." Felice wanted to grab the notepad, but had to keep winding. She did her best to memorize the frequencies. "I'll leave you with some music. It should last until morning. Good night, and God bless, whatever form He might take."

She put the radio on the bed for a moment to write down the information, then powered it up again. She hoped some easy listening music would help relax Mikey—and herself, if she were willing to admit it. She expected the DJ to play something soft and sad, morose or respectful.

Sunshine, Lollipops and Rainbows was pretty much the opposite. Yet somehow it was the perfect song. There were others out there. People trying to help and not just hide in a bunker. People who were organized, or organizing. Right now that made all the difference. The song put a smile on her face, and when she looked at Mikey, she saw his head bobbing left and right.

Not quite knowing why, Felice got up and began to dance, singing part of the lyrics.

Mikey didn't join in, but watched her dance while she cranked the radio, and swayed in time with the tune. Felice's dancing got progressively sillier, holding the radio like her dance partner and twirling like mad for an audience of one.

When the song ended she was fell onto the chair in a heap, exhausted and dizzy. The radio died. She giggled, even though her arm had started cramping. She could see herself in the mirror; her dark hair frazzled and uniform an absolute mess. She wondered how the hell she had become a cop in the first place. Clearly the stage had been her true calling.

It was getting dark fast now. She lit one of the candles and told Mikey to get ready for bed. This consisted of Mikey getting into bed without taking anything off, and Felice doing the same. Taking off her clothes in front of a nine year old who wasn't her son? She'd have to arrest herself—again. But neither had a change of clothes, something of which she made a note for her next trip into town.

"Do you want me to tell you a story?" she asked. It seemed like the thing to do, and, it turned out, she could remember quite a few. Not that it mattered, because Mikey was already fast asleep. She blew out the candle.

"Maybe next time."

The festival in Görlitzhafen did not end because the sun went down. Great fires were lit and much dancing and carousing remained to be had. She found one of her sisters talking and laughing with a man headed for the great stage, where people were busy putting the set together for the evening's performance. He called her Lia as he bade her farewell.

Her sister was more than a little surprised to see her.

"You were allowed to enter?"

"After a fashion."

Lia no doubt knew exactly what she meant. "I see. Well, I'm pleased to see you. It wasn't right, you alone not receiving an invitation."

On that point they agreed, but she had no desire to talk about it. "You call yourself Lia now?"

Her sister smiled. "Formality and titles should mean nothing here, don't you think? Such things would only get in the way."

"Of course."

In the distance, the king's magician lit the night sky with magic sparks that flew and exploded in every direction. Lia laughed and applauded with the audience. From his podium, the duke raised his hands to silence those nearby. He was about to announce awards of valor for a number of knights in attendance.

"Amazing, is it not?"

She nodded to Lia, but said nothing.

Her sister then gestured to the stage. "I will be performing as well later tonight."

"You must be excited."

"I am. It's been a long time. And what, pray tell, will you be doing?"

"I'm certain I can keep myself entertained." And with that she turned and walked away.

By a tavern at the outer wall, she found a comely lad who had the bearing of a noble's son, or perhaps a wealthy merchant. Either way, he had power. Importance. Name and title. She smiled and walked seductively toward him in tall, half-boots that featured her painted toes.

It didn't take long to get his ear, and not many words to get him all to herself. In a few minutes, they were kissing and caressing behind a stable. She felt his warmth on her body, his hands searching for flesh. She knew what he wanted, and he had what she desired.

With a flourish, she hopped up and wrapped her legs around his waist. Caught off guard, his legs wobbled a little before he recovered. She grabbed him by the head, locked her eyes onto his and said in an alluring voice, "Who are you?"

The boy smiled, perhaps realizing they had gone a little fast, even by festival standards. "I am Kalen, son of Sir Roland, right hand of the Duke."

"Tell me about yourself."

"And what would you have me tell you, my lady?"

She let out a deep sigh that barely contained her longing. "*Everything.*"

Day 3

Felice awoke feeling great for the first time in as long as she could remember—which admittedly was only three days. They had food, equipment, and contact with the outside world, even if it was one way. Running water would be nice; she would kill for a hot shower, but for now she'd settle for the sun on her face. She opened the curtain to let the light in.

The dead stockbroker stood outside the window, his face like a bowling ball painted by Salvador Dali. His head tilted and looked straight at Felice.

"Shit!" She jumped back and scrambled to the night stand to grab the shotgun. The ruckus woke Mikey up; he rubbed sleep from his eyes, but didn't seem to comprehend what was going on. By the time Felice loaded a shell and turned back to the window the man was no longer there. "Shit!" Mikey looked up at her. "Stay there." She said it calmly, hoping not to panic the poor kid.

Leaving through the front door would be stupid. He'd expect that, and even with the Glock they'd start off at grappling range. No, not he. It. It had taken only a second or two of face sucking to doom that man, and there was nothing left of him now. She wouldn't let the same thing happen to her or the kid. She went to the bathroom fire escape window and started pulling it open when a deep voice moaned at the front door.

"*Bumblebum...*"

Felice's heart stopped. Time slowed as she ran back to the bedroom. Mikey was obediently reaching for the door knob.

Stupid, stupid kid.

With one hand, she grabbed the back of his school uniform and tossed him onto the bed, but his hand had been on the handle. The door opened. With a sure grip, she shoved the barrel of her shotgun into one of the stockbroker's empty eye sockets, voids that held no surprise, only despair.

"It's *Mister* Bumblebum," said Felice.

The shot was muffled, like it had been fired miles away, and did absolutely nothing. Even the recoil was weak; given how she held the gun, it should have dislocated her shoulder. The thing pushed its way into the room. The barrel thrust so deep it should have burst through the back of its head. The stockbroker reached for Felice. She dropped the shotgun, gripped the thing's throat with her left hand, drew her sidearm with her right, and fired three shots into its belly. The stockbroker staggered back. She raised the Glock and fired three more times, aiming for center of mass. The thing tripped and fell onto the parking lot.

Felice looked at the shotgun on the ground. It had been in the stockbroker's head half way up to the trigger. That wasn't possible. She holstered the Glock and picked it up. The barrel was steaming, but not from heat. The pump was freezing cold. She checked on Mikey, who was in so much shock it seemed all the progress they'd made these last two days had been undone.

"Are you okay?"

Mikey didn't answer.

"Stay."

He wasn't going anywhere.

Felice walked to the body on the parking lot. It was still moving. It wasn't bleeding. Looking back, neither had the one in the city. The thing on the ground had six holes in its abdomen, but there was only gray ash instead of blood. Its arms reached toward the motel door.

"*Must...take care...*"

Felice gasped. Something inside had held onto the information she'd given. The password, the location of the boy. A fragment of the person was still in there, lost in the torment reflected on its face. Perhaps on some level it even thought it had come to help.

She corrected herself. No, not it. He.

Gordon.

"I'm sorry."

She leveled the shotgun and fired. The stockbroker's chest burst into an ashen cloud. What was left didn't move. She could see the back of his skull through the eye sockets now. They no longer held an endless void within them. They were just empty.

Felice went back to her room, shut the door, and dropped in a heap. Her head sagged. All at once she began to cry, using the now-warm barrel of the shotgun like a crutch to hold herself up. She didn't know the man, she had only spoken a few words to him. Why did she feel like this?

He had been so helpless, and Felice hadn't been able to save him, or even give him comfort. Everything about the situation was inhuman. She couldn't begin to fathom how any of this could be allowed to happen, and didn't want to live in a world where she could. If the only thing waiting for her out there was more of the moaning damned, what was the point of going on?

A small hand rested on her shoulder. Mikey knelt down beside Felice and gave her the same kind of hug she had given him last night. She opened her eyes. Looking down at her chest, she saw his face reflected like a funhouse mirror in one of her silver badge's points. This was about duty. Not the duty of a police officer, something more fundamental than that. She looked up and took Mikey's hand. Smiled. Held it tight.

"Must take care."

She used the red wagon to drag the stockbroker's body and the shovel far behind the motel. It was barely morning and already the worst day yet. The parts of the man's body that had been shot flaked and blew away in the wind. Ashes to ashes, dust to dust; Gordon was already a bit of both. The head looked like it had been replaced with paper mache. She knew those changes went right down to the bone, like the corpses in the restaurant. She reckoned they needed a burial, too. Later. She took the shovel, stuck it in the dry ground, and began digging.

When she was done, she didn't give a prayer. She didn't think anyone would be listening. She only said, "I'm sorry" again, and left it at that.

❧

Mikey was on the floor, rolling two red and white fishing bobbers that she had dug out of the knapsack like marbles, trying to knock one with the other. Felice smiled to herself. *Fact of life: kids get bored. World goes to hell in a handbasket and once things quiet down a bit they say, "Are we there yet?" Then you try playing some music to shut them up while you worry about—*

Felice gasped. The radio. It was well past when the DJ said he'd start broadcasting. She grabbed the flashlight/radio and began cranking.

"...seems to be down again from this time yesterday. I'm hoping that means you all are getting better at hiding from the Moaners, and not because...well, pretty much any other scenario I can think of. That's the WTHH traffic report, now let's move onto Weather—clear and hot, despite those dark clouds over the mountains. Long range forecast—not a clue. And now Sports—none. Entertainment—you're listening to it. Science and Technology—nothing Doc McKay is willing to share. Moving on to International News: still no comment from China on whether this is some kind of biological warfare attack. But it's not as if anyone can exactly call us to tell us if it is. So that leaves us with Local News.

"A shout out goes to the plucky lady police officer who tried to save someone from a Moaner attack yesterday. We got word of this last night from our only confirmed listener outside of Haven. It happened out by the pile up on South Main. She put the Moaner down, but unfortunately the victim didn't make it. I don't know where this lady of the law holes up, there ain't much outside city limits, but I hope she's paying attention and keeping both eyes peeled, because according to our listener, she didn't finish the job."

"Thanks for the warning," Felice grumbled.

"I guess she hasn't figured out how things work, but it's a hell of a crash course we're all taking, and fate doesn't grade on a curve. Not everyone can get the job done the way Agent Groves can. He's brought ten more people to Haven last night. How that man does it I have no idea, but he's a hero to us all."

Felice suddenly liked the DJ a lot less. Talk about damned with faint praise. "Fuck you."

Mikey looked at her.

"I mean, *darn* you. Darn. Darn it. Darn it to heck."

Her arm was already getting tired; she had been digging after all. She handed the radio to Mikey to keep winding, then took out her notepad and began to take notes.

Haven. Survivors are gathering there. Where is it?
Agent Groves. Must know more than me. Agent of what?
Doc McKay. For real or DJ joke?

On the radio, the DJ tried to be reassuring, sending messages from those in Haven who hoped to make contact with loved ones they prayed were still out there somewhere.

"For those new to WTHH radio, we can't risk giving the location of Haven over the air. As far as we know, Moaners aren't smart but they seem to remember things. If anyone taken by them knew where we are, that would be big trouble. I'm sorry; that's just the way things are. We've already had two minor attacks by what might have been scouts trying to find our entrance, or just mindless wanderers. We're not taking any chances. Right now Agent Groves is our go-to guy out on the streets. You see a red flag; it's him or someone he trusts. They'll help you get to Haven."

Felice scribbled *Red Flag* next to her Haven note, with an arrow pointing to Agent Groves.

"And now a moment for Moaner Safety. *Know your enemy.* As

much as this might seem like some kind of zombie apocalypse, we've seen time and again that shooting the head does little or nothing. The back of the head seems to work, but if you see them, chances are they see you. If you have a weapon, aim for the chest. If you can't get a gun, find anything that has reach on it, like a pitchfork. That will allow you to push them back, keep them at arm's length. If you can't get one of those, find a broomstick handle and duct tape a kitchen knife on the end. Do whatever it takes to keep them from getting close."

She didn't bother writing any of this down, as those lessons had been burned into her brain the hard way. There were some muffled noises on the radio. Felice wondered if Mikey wasn't cranking hard enough.

"Okay, Yuri's telling me we need to move the antenna again. Don't touch that dial, we're going to be off the air for an hour or two. Be prepared, stay safe, and God bless." A few moments later the station went to static. Felice took the radio from the boy.

"Get dressed," she said before remembering he already was, more or less. "Er...put on your hat. We're going on a road trip."

Felice wasn't sure taking Mikey back to Fort Rock was a good idea, but *was* sure leaving him in the motel wasn't. She didn't know if these "Moaners" communicated or followed one another's trails like ants, but there was no way she could protect him unless he tagged along, and to prevent him from panicking it was important to keep things light.

"We're going shopping, get some more chocolate, find you some hip new clothes. All right?" Mikey looked down at his outfit, as if he had trouble grasping the concept that his current school attire was un-hip, or perhaps trying to figure out what hip meant.

Felice took the notepad and made a list of things they'd need. The knapsack had a detachable daypack, in which she stuffed food, water, the flashlight/radio, first aid kit and a flare gun, along with other odds and ends just in case. Nothing too heavy.

Her plan, if she could call it that, was to find one of those red flags and get Mikey into Haven. It sounded like the survivors were organized. Mikey would be safe and she could try and help this Agent Groves person. She could always come back to the motel for the rest of the supplies.

It wasn't so much a plan as a goal, but she could live with that.

"All right, kiddo. Adventure, ho! You ride the bike, I'll bring the wagon."

Mikey froze the moment they stepped outside. Felice frowned. She realized he hadn't left the room since he'd arrived—well, aside from one time with the shovel and a roll of toilet paper. It might have hit him: he was leaving the only place he considered safe. Then she followed his gaze. He was staring at the bike.

"What's wrong?" Mikey didn't answer. He must know how to ride one—what nine year old didn't? "Look, I left the wagon around back. Why don't you try the bike out in the parking lot while I go get it?"

She was halfway back when she heard a crash. She rushed to the lot and saw the bike on its side, Mikey on the pavement, clutching his ankle.

"Ow..."

Felice knelt beside him. "Are you all right? Can you get up?" He tried, but limped and whimpered. "You might have sprained it." She looked at the sun. She wanted to make the most of the day.

"I've got an idea."

She hooked the wagon to the bike as she had before, and had Mikey sit in it. Felice wore the daypack with the shotgun strapped on. Fortunately, the road was flat and it wasn't hard dragging him behind. Poor kid, probably so excited at the idea of riding a bike again he tried a stunt and fell over. After all, every boy considered a bicycle to be one step away from a motorcycle: the ultimate in cool. Even if it was pink...

Felice slammed on the brakes. They were about half way to the pile-up and she cursed herself for taking so long to figure things out.

"Okay, smart guy. Your turn to ride."

Mikey got out of the wagon and began to limp.

"Nice try, but it was the other leg."

Mikey shifted his weight to the other side.

"I'm sorry, I was lying. You were right the first time."

Mikey shifted back.

"Give it up, you're busted. No one's going to make fun of you for riding a pink bike, even one with tassles."

Mikey reluctantly got on.

"Good boy. We're getting closer to the city. I need my hands free if I'm going to protect you. And if anything happens you need to ride away as fast as possible. Understood?" Felice unhitched the wagon and dragged it behind her, putting in her gear for easy access.

At times, Mikey would bike slowly to keep up with her. Sometimes he would speed ahead, circle around and come back, but he always looked afraid that at any moment someone would point and laugh at him. Felice couldn't help but smile. First tricking her into chauffeuring him and now this? Aside from overloading on junk food, it was the most normal child behavior she'd seen from him.

When they reached the pile-up, she had Mikey swing wide off road. She paid more attention to what she saw this time. She noticed a few baked bodies still had Moaner eyes, though most were half-crumpled to dust. The ash on the street hadn't shifted from before. Still no wind.

"Come back, Mikey. Don't go too far."

The boy circled back, standing on the pedals to gain momentum on the grassland. They passed what was left of the strip club, then through burnt out suburbia—such as it was—and made their first intended stop at the hermit's bunker.

Felice rapped the window—soft, then hard. "Open up, police!" she said at last, not that it had meant anything the first time.

The slot on the green door slid open, but no barrel was shoved into her face. The eyes peeking out were narrow. "You interrupted ma musin's," he grunted, and then looked her over. "Still alive, eh? Congrats. Now git. I helped all I could."

Felice waved to the sidewalk. Mikey stood there, having discarded the girl's bike several yards away so as not to be associated with it. "Look, I just wanted to show you that I wasn't lying to you. I can take care of myself, but this is a real boy who needs real help. If you can't help us, maybe you can at least tell us how to get to Haven."

The hermit's eyes widened at the name, then narrowed. The hermit looked Felice over, then the boy. "Is that a school uniform the boy's wearin?"

Felice had no idea why that was relevant but said, "Yes."

The hermit hummed in thought. "Wait there." The slot slid shut. Locks, bolts, and chains rattled down the side of the door, which then opened.

"Git in before they see you."

Felice waved Mikey inside and followed behind, bringing the daypack with her.

The first thing she noticed was the hermit was nowhere near

as tall as the eye slit had suggested. He was shorter than Mikey. The next thing was the hermit wasn't a he, but a she. Either that or he was taking some serious hormone therapy. The squat wizened woman resembled a wrinkled pear with an ample bosom.

"You don't want to find Haven," she said, her deep voice easily mistaken for a man's. "Believe me. Where did you say yer stayin now?" The woman waddled over to the counter. The interior of the store was pretty much what Felice expected: part camping goods, part hunting, part government paranoia. The lights were on; she heard a generator somewhere.

"A motel by the city limits."

The hermit nodded. "Good spot, good spot. Now, you take my advice and go back. The end will come all the same, but you be more comfortable out there. Best for you. Best for the boy. Take what you need and go back till then."

Felice frowned. The woman's fatalism was hardly inspiring. "I'm not about to give up, ma'am, and neither should you. If there's a chance—"

"Chance?" The crone's laugh came out like a croak. "There is no chance. Only time." She went behind the counter and jotted a few things down in a hardcover notebook before closing the cover. She put the notebook under the register and replaced it with a larger book, bound in leather. "Time that is running out."

"Then what's the point?"

"Exactly."

Felice walked away before she lost her temper and browsed the equipment in the store. Mikey had already ditched his school jacket and was trying on t-shirts with slogans like *Kill em all and let God sort em out*; *All I need is an Uzi, a Floozy, and a Jacuzzi*; and the unforgettable classic *Nuke em till they glow, then shoot em in the dark!* They had a selection of practical outdoor clothing as well, and Felice picked out a couple of shirts and pants in her size.

As they shopped, the old woman began reading in a calm, stoic voice. Felice tried to tune it out and get on with things, but her ears picked up odd little snippets now and then.

"It was judged that he was much better qualified to execute what was now required, rather than to remain and defend, with courage and ability, this lair most remarkably fortified by the hand of man."

She looked at the shoes and boots. Hers were a mess; maybe

she could find something more comfortable.

"...the general chose his three most trusted soldiers to accompany him into battle."

Hiking boots? No. She was sick of heavy shoes. Something lighter. Was it just her, or had the old woman lost her rustic accent?

"...the fortress wall stretched from east to west, with towers at an interval of three hundred feet, which, at its front, was contracted to a road capable of admitting only a single carriage."

She grabbed a couple of pairs without thinking. She wished that woman would shut up!

"...the troops that had been posted to defend the carriage remained, awaiting the return of the general with the healer."

She couldn't ignore it any more. Curiosity was an itch that had to be scratched. "What the heck are you reading?"

Her accent returned. "*The Decline and Fall of the Roman Empire.* We're comin to the fall."

"That didn't sound like —" She was cut off by Mikey, now wearing a "*Better Dead Than Red*" shirt and a camouflage jacket, holding up a chocolate bar for her approval.

"So you'll take whatever clothes you want, but ask permission for a chocolate bar? Nothing wrong with your moral compass. Go ask the crazy lady of it's okay."

Mikey ran over to the counter with the bar. She began revising her Hansel and Gretel theory. The only safe secure house in a hostile wilderness, full of candy and supplies, with an old crone keeping watch? Maybe there were some similarities after all.

"Oh, I embellish, of course," said the hermit, ruffling Mikey's hair and giving him two more chocolate bars from the display rack. "This revised edition lacks the flare of the original. I coulda read from the Book of Revelation, but that's a bit, whachacallit, *klee-shay.*"

"Look, ma'am. Sorry I called you crazy. I'm grateful you're letting us get supplies, but as bad as this is, I refuse to give up because you think the bible says so."

The hermit laughed. "Oh, not the bible, deary. *History.* I have all the history I need here." She thumped the floor with the butt of her shotgun, as if to proclaim lordship over all she surveyed. "That way I kin see it all comin, agin and agin."

Felice was about to take back her apology but thought better of it. She picked up a duffle bag for the clothes and other equipment, including the daypack.

"Thank you for letting us take these things. Are you sure it's all right?"

"Of course. Take as much as you need. As much as you need. Jes 'cause it's the end of the world doesn't mean we shouldn't act charitable to one another."

Felice frowned. "You don't have an extra large oven in the basement by any chance, do you?"

"Pardon?"

"Nothing. It's just that wasn't your attitude yesterday. Hell, it wasn't your attitude ten minutes ago."

The wrinkled woman winked. "That's because I didn' know you. Now I do, or, at least, I *think* I do. Come agin if you're not dead. If you are, stay the hell away. I'd hate to blow a hole through ya." The hermit peeked through the blinds behind the bulletproof window and clucked in disapproval.

"Ah, jes some lost souls out there. Musta heard ya come in. Jes a moment." She placed a footstool by the door, got up, opened the slide, and opened fire with her shotgun. Felice covered Mikey's ears, but most of the noise was outside. They heard the empty moans get closer as the hermit reloaded, then opened fire again.

"All clear. You best git a move on." She went to the back room and returned with a red gas can, then unlocked the door. "Don't come back till tomorrow at the earliest, y'hear?"

Felice nodded. As they left, the old woman doused the bodies and their hollow faces with gasoline, weaving a path from one corpse to the next. She waited until Felice and Mikey were well away before lighting the trail and shutting the door. Felice wondered if she needed to revisit the body behind the motel that night, just to be safe. The DJ hadn't mentioned burning in his safety tips. Maybe he didn't know.

Despite the hermit's advice, she had no intention of going back to the motel. Not yet. Haven was out there, and it had to be the best place for Mikey. She pictured it as a secured second floor in one of the larger buildings, something easily barricaded with room to expand going up, the ground floor stairs demolished, but low enough so escape through the windows on all sides was possible. There was a question as to how active and thinking these Moaners were. They weren't zombies—zombies didn't have endless abysses inside their skulls—but shared certain traits, such as an absence of personality and retaining only a primeval behavior. Felice didn't rightly care one way or the other.

"Grab your Harley, Mikey. Time to go."

She left the duffle bag and wagon near the hermit's bunker. They'd pick them up on the way back if they weren't successful. They had something to eat, then headed for the downtown core, which seemed to her as foreign and dangerous as any jungle.

It was hard to say if they were better off in the middle of the road where they were more visible but could see all comers, or to the side where they'd be better concealed but vulnerable to ambush. She chose the former, keeping the boy on his bike close.

The city was dead. Whatever had hit this place seemed to be long gone. There weren't even any bodies. Every car they saw was smashed, burned, or otherwise wrecked, but there weren't many around to begin with. Perhaps most of the town evacuated. This couldn't be the only road out of the city.

It was funny how her knowledge of the world grew only as she moved within it. She kept expecting something to trigger a memory and make all of Fort Rock familiar to her. Instead, it always felt like she was seeing each place for the first time.

Like the bowling alley in front of them. It was perfectly iconic with its oversized billboard depicting knocked-over pins. The sign stood out from the surrounding drab, ordinary buildings, and was impossible not to notice, right by two major streets. How could she not remember it?

Of course, she was a *state* trooper. Maybe she'd never been to Fort Rock before.

Felice heard something in the distance and waved Mikey to stop. It was getting closer, whatever it was. Erring on the side of caution, she picked the boy up off his bike and hid behind a truck that had smashed into a lamppost. She kept Mikey in front so they could watch from a crouched position.

The dead streets came to life. She heard moans in every direction, even behind them.

Behind them?

Felice turned her head. A half dozen Moaners were approaching. In the second it took to choose between fight and flight, she realized they weren't looking at her at all, but were walking toward the bowling alley.

She held Mikey still, her hand over his mouth, and waited for them to pass. Only when the last one walked by did she look to see where they were going. More had passed on the opposite side of the road, and still more had come from other directions.

And then they stopped. In scattered spots around the intersection they stopped, spaced perhaps a few yards apart. The closest was right in front of their truck, making Felice reluctant to flee.

What the hell was going on? Were they going to do the Thriller dance? Was this some kind of Moaner social mixer?

Hey, Bob, how you doin? Still a vacuous abomination? Me too! Remember when we both got our souls sucked out? Good times. Feed on any survivors lately? I got a lawyer yesterday, not much there, let me tell you.

The roar of a car engine interrupted her thoughts. A black four-door sedan screeched around the corner to the far north at high speed. It fish tailed into two Moaners, knocking them into a wall, which blasted them to dust. The vehicle then righted itself and drove toward Felice and Mikey. A red flag waved from a rear window.

As if on cue, every Moaner in the area was drawn to the car. Some ran while others walked. The sedan knocked them aside or ran them over easily enough at first, but their numbers were so dense the vehicle soon slowed. Bodies jumped onto the hood and grabbed at the windows. The car spun around, stopping in front of the bowling alley, though the laws of motion meant the Moaners on top just kept on going, some leaving arms behind.

The streets echoed with gunfire as bursts of flame poured from every car window. Moaners dropped and dust flew until the immediate area was clear. Four men and one woman piled out of the vehicle, the men carrying everything from pistols to assault rifles. The unarmed woman wore a bloodied lab coat and glasses. One of the men—the one with the assault rifle—had a dark blue FBI jacket on, while the others were dressed in civilian clothes.

For the first time in three days, Felice had a feeling of recognition.

Or was it déjà vu?

The FBI man barked to the others. "Terry, cover the north road, there's more coming! Jasper, Neil, stick with the Doc! *Go! Go! Go!* Get inside!"

All hell broke loose. The air rang with gunfire and ricochets. Felice nodded to herself. This was where she was needed.

"Stay close behind me, Mikey. We're going to help."

She started to rise, but the boy pulled her back down, shaking his head.

"Mikey, don't argue. This is important. They know where Haven is, and they can keep you safe. Now come on."

Mikey refused to get up. Felice pulled him to his feet, but he dropped down again. "Don't make me carry you!"

"No! She'll be coming!" Mikey covered his mouth, his eyes wide open, as if he'd just told a terrible secret.

Felice frowned. "Who?" Mikey shook his head. Felice heard another car coming. "*Who?*"

A moment later, a candy apple red Ferrari pulled to a stop at the intersection. None of the Moaners made a move toward it. In fact, they all stood still again. No more gunfire came from the bowling alley. It was as if the whole world—or at least a two-block radius of it—held its breath.

The Ferrari door opened. A tall black leather half-boot with the toes cut out stepped onto the asphalt. A woman, possibly in her thirties, climbed out. She had fiery red hair and was dressed in what Felice considered an entirely inappropriate black outfit that left little to the imagination. She walked toward the bowling alley, taking the time to pat a couple Moaners on the head like cherished pets.

"We have to go," said Mikey. Felice was inclined to agree, but couldn't take her eyes off the woman. The déjà vu had returned. She'd seen her before. Where? She kept thinking of a name… one that sounded like Hell.

Someone threw a rock at her from the bowling alley. The woman paid no attention as it lobbed over her head and landed under the sports car.

It wasn't a rock.

The car exploded, buckling from underneath and jumping ten feet in the air. A dozen Moaners were knocked down by the blast, but all it did to the woman was blow her hair around like in a shampoo commercial.

Mikey tugged on her arm. "We have to go *now.*" Felice had a bad feeling bullets would just piss this woman off. She nodded and began to fall back.

As if hoping to prove her wrong, the people in the bowling alley opened fire. Moaners on either side of the hell-woman danced like epileptics at a disco and dropped in heaps of ash. The woman in black staggered under the withering fire and fell over. Once again, the streets held their breath.

The woman got up and brushed the flattened lead off her like bugs on a windscreen.

"That hurt!" she yelled.

That settled it. Time to go.

Just as Felice turned, there was a crash of glass. She looked back in time to see a Harley Davidson leap through a large picture window on one side of the bowling alley, a *'Grand Prize'* banner flapping behind it. The FBI guy drove, while the 'Doc' held onto him for dear life. The others had been left behind to fend off the Moaners and the hell-woman as long as possible.

Felice had trouble processing what she'd just seen, and fled with Mikey as the gunfire erupted once again. She had experienced three new kinds of bat-shit insanity in the last five minutes and was not eager for a fourth.

The journey home was mostly traveled in a daze. At the edge of consciousness Felice had seen...what? She knew what she saw, but to acknowledge it would grant those images a validity they didn't deserve. So her mind rebelled, insisting she had *not* seen what she most assuredly *had*.

She had not seen dozens of Moaners arrange themselves like...

She had not seen a black sedan drive like...

She had not seen four men shooting like...

She had not seen the Hell-woman show up like...

She couldn't finish any of those sentences. Her brain kicked the thoughts out and demanded un-tampered data.

She felt like this all the way back to the motel. She didn't even have the presence of mind to pick up their gear near the hermit's bunker. Mikey had to remind her.

Mikey. That was another can of worms her brain wouldn't let her open yet. *She'll be coming*, he'd said. Those words implied a world of possibilities. Mikey, for his part, had gone back to his silent routine. Routine. She already didn't trust the little bugger. Perhaps on some level, he knew.

They passed by the pile-up and made the long trip to the motel in silence.

"Home sweet home," she said at last. They were at the ruined diner, no sign of unwelcome visitors. That was something, at least.

In their room, she unloaded the duffle bag and sorted the new gear and clothing. When she got to the shoes, she discovered she had grabbed a couple pairs of moccasins instead of running shoes, most likely in her frustration with the hermit lady. She frowned. At least they were compact.

With that out of the way, she had two choices. Confront the nonsense that had been heaped on her today, or find a new outlet for her denial.

"Who's up for a nice game of Parcheesi?" Mikey looked at her, confused. Felice sighed. "Doesn't matter, I don't even know how to play." She looked at the boy. Might as well get it over with.

"You said, 'She'll be coming.' Who is 'she'? How did you know?"

She expected Mikey to go into another panic, like when she

asked about his family, or go back to a catatonic state, but he didn't. Instead, he went to the nightstand and pulled out the Gideon bible. He handed it to her.

Felice didn't get it. What was he trying to say? She was pretty sure the Good Book didn't cover soul-sucking vacuum headed zombies or sluttily dressed hell-women who were immune to gunfire. Call it a hunch. But Mikey's eyes were insistent.

"All right, fine. Where should I start?" Mikey opened the cover for her. "In the Beginning, huh?" She remembered that the first few pages had been missing and Genesis started at Chapter 3. She looked at the page. Her eyes widened as she scanned the opening passage.

She slammed the book shut.

"The hell was that?" The boy didn't have answers, but she could see he knew what she had seen. "Did you read this?"

Mikey nodded. He pointed at the blank TV screen and said, "You said it would rot my brain."

And this was the only thing to read in the room. Felice's heart beat faster. Most of her was saying now was a *really* good time to learn Parcheesi, but a small screaming part of her demanded she open the cover again, and she obeyed.

This was not the Genesis she remembered.

CHAPTER 3

Fort Rock, Agent David Groves decided, had been christened after one of the more unimaginatively named old west outposts in American History. It was a small city in northwestern America, about twenty thousand people. Maybe it had a future, maybe it didn't. He didn't rightly care.

2. He mentioned his theory to his partner, Eric, who took out his iPhone and quickly proved him wrong. Fort Rock was named after the quarry that had been its lifeblood for fifty years.

3. "The town pretty much died after World War I, then found new life during World War II when a steel factory opened. And recently they added a maximum security prison." He snorted. "Just in time for World War III."

4. "Thank you, Doctor Google," said Groves. He drove past the city limits sign, next to an old single level motel strip. The arrow on its sign pointed down, afraid you might miss it. "You ever try coming up with theories without resorting to Wikipedia? The ancient Greeks used to debate how many teeth were in a horse's head without ever checking."

5. Eric looked as if his partner had told him the sun had been formed by combining Mentos and cola. "What the hell is the point of that?"

6. Groves sighed. "It's the debate that mattered. Letting everyone contribute to it. If you had looked out the window and saw an old rock quarry over there and brought it up as a theory, that would be one thing. That would tell me something about you, how you think. But looking on the internet? You checked the horse's teeth."

7. "You don't think the fact I did some research tells you something about me?"

8. "It tells me you're the sort of person who always lets other people tell you what to think."

9. Eric turned off his phone. "They warned me about you, you know."

10. Groves smiled, his eyes hidden under his sunglasses. "They did, huh?"

11. "Yeah."

12. "Good."

13. They let it drop there. Groves had a reputation in the Bureau as a bit of an oddball. People talked about him as if he went with his gut instincts alone, that he was about the psychological rather than the factual.

14. Eric had been assigned as Groves's partner only a few hours before they'd gotten in the car. He was shorter than Groves, with darker hair, and narrow rectangular glasses that made him look like a desk jockey out of his element. Groves planned on reading Eric's file tonight, but could already tell his marriage was on shaky ground, he had one child, had been an A student, and had only become a full

field agent in the last six months.

15. Not that Eric had volunteered any of this. Until now, the only personal information they'd shared were favorite baseball teams.

16. They passed a trucker's strip club. The neon sign was off. His gaze drifted up to the woman on her back with one leg straight up and the other bent at an angle. Groves reflected a moment about the finer things in life.

17. Fort Rock Penitentiary was on the other side of town, forcing them to drive through what passed for a business center. A few big office buildings, outnumbered by mom and pop stores that would dry up and blow away the moment Wal-Mart decided to drop a mall in range. The building that somehow felt like it most belonged was a bowling alley. No name on the sign on the roof (also neon) just pins getting smashed by a ball. It summed up the city to a tee.

18. Ten minutes later, they pulled up to the guardhouse by the outer perimeter of the penitentiary. IDs were checked and they were allowed to pass. The warden waited in a golf cart at the visitor's parking lot. Hardly prison issue, and it certainly hadn't helped the warden cut down on his waistline. They shook hands. The warden introduced himself as Terry Casso, and the two agents got in the back of the cart.

19. "Glad you could make it. I was beginning to worry."

20. "Worry?" The choice of words interested Groves. They couldn't have been that late.

21. "That some jackass up the line changed their minds and we'd be stuck with her for god knows how much longer. She doesn't belong here." Groves looked at the middle fence as they drove past, clearly marked with lethal current warnings.

22. "That's why we're here," said Agent Groves.

Fort Rock. Agent Groves. Motel. Strip club. Bowling alley...
The book fell from Felice's hand.

She *had* seen dozens of Moaners arrange themselves *like pieces on a set.*

She *had* seen a black sedan drive *like a stuntman was at the wheel.*

She *had* seen four men shooting *like they were in an action movie.*

She *had* seen the Hell-woman show up *like the main villain making an entrance.*

"This is a story."

When confronted with the impossible, it is perfectly natural to suddenly believe what you are seeing is really there *and* look for the man behind the curtain at the same time. Sure the woman in the magic act looks like she's floating, but those wires had to be hidden *somewhere*.

Felice picked up the book and kept reading. She flipped to The Book of Revelation and the text was—as far as she could tell—normal, with seals and pale horses and second comings and all the rest.

Jumping about halfway back, it talked about Agent Groves again. She scanned the pages in rapid succession, mentally blocking out the annoying biblical formatting, trying to find where the story ended and the bible began, when she came across something all too familiar.

> ...Groves slammed the brakes and swerved the sedan, knocking several Moaners down, then gunned the engine. There were too many of them; they were slowing him with sheer numbers. They wouldn't get much farther, and *she* wasn't far behind.
>
> He spotted a bowling alley up ahead; it was the only place they might be able to put up some kind of defense—if they could get there.
>
> "We're going to fight our way inside, got it?" Terry and the others nodded, ready for action. "Stay close, Doc. When we move, you move."
>
> Liz frowned. No one ever seemed to take her seriously. "I'm not a child, Agent Groves, you don't have to—"
>
> "Great story, Doc. Tell me the rest later." He stopped the car outside the entrance. Groves grabbed his rifle and all four men opened fire...

Felice read every word carefully. Everything she had seen was right there in black and white and third person omniscient, along with a lot she hadn't: the battle to get into the bowling alley, barricading themselves inside, creating a defensive perimeter, Groves arguing with the Doc. And then—

"G-man!" Neil called out. "We have a situation! They've stopped moving!"

Groves strode to the entrance as a red Ferrari pulled up. He didn't need to see the driver to know they were in trouble.

"The bitch is back."

"I thought we lost her back at the prison," said Neil.

Groves knew better. He watched her pat a couple of Moaners like favorite pets. "With those things around we'll never be able to lose her. Damn!"

"Wonderful escape plan," said Liz. "Instead of dying in a prison hospital, I get to die trapped in a building full of unsanitary shoes." Next to Groves, they were her least favorite things here.

"Not now, Doc."

"She's right, though," said Jasper. "We're screwed."

Terry pulled out a grenade. "Yeah, well, let's see how she likes this." He chucked it out the window before Groves could stop him.

"Where the hell did you get that?" he barked.

Terry shrugged. "Birthday present."

The Ferrari exploded into the air, but just as he feared, it had no effect on Mel...

Mel. *That* was her name. And somehow she knew she had met her before, but where? She had to go back to the beginning. She had to know how this all started.

For now, the impossible was accepted. She was in a story. Fine. Moving on.

But now that her understanding of reality had been shattered to the core, existential questions like "Who am I?" and "Why am I here?" suddenly took on a new urgency and importance.

Felice began to think she had been central to what was going on. Maybe she had been working with Groves before she got amnesia and he needed her help for this nightmare to end. Maybe he was out there looking for her.

She flipped back to where she'd left off in Chapter 3.

"Glad you could make it. I was beginning to worry."

"Worry?" The choice of words interested Groves. They couldn't have been that late.

"That some jackass up the line changed their minds and we'd be stuck with her for god knows how much longer. She doesn't belong here." Groves looked at the middle fence as they drove past, which was clearly marked with lethal current warnings.

"That's why we're here," said Agent Groves.

"Yes, well, you can understand my concern. ADX doesn't have women inmates."

"This is an exceptional case," said Eric.

Warden Casso nodded as they reached the main gate. "You got that right."

They got out of the cart and entered the main building on foot. Fort Rock was a large high security prison; over ten percent of the city's population was made up of the guards, support staff, and their families.

Their first stop was the Warden's office, painted in cool, soothing colors. They went through the usual niceties, going out of their way to make sure no one in the room had a bigger dick than anyone else. Casso and Eric briefly discussed the current standoff with China.

"Like we don't have enough problems," said Casso. "Now it looks like China's going to make their move."

"It's just sword rattling," said Eric. "Be over in a week. Taiwan's not worth it."

The warden drummed his fingers on the table. "That's not how CNN's calling it." Again, Groves noticed little things about Casso's manners that didn't quite fit. Despite the talk of war, his mind was only on one thing—he couldn't wait to get rid of the bitch. For him to be more frightened of her than all out war with China was saying something.

Casso escorted them to the women's facility. Groves glanced at the subject's file on his phone. Mel Doe. Even now they didn't know her last name. He scrolled down. The mug shot was of a middle-aged woman, probably smoking hot twenty years back; long red hair, and the faintest smug look on her lips he'd ever seen anyone pull off. To the casual observer it would appear completely neutral. Maybe he was projecting into the image.

There was nothing in the file he hadn't read before. How she hadn't been found legally insane was beyond him; how she hadn't been sentenced to death even more so.

Warden Casso nodded to a guard, who buzzed them into the maximum-security wing. Here, prisoners had individual cells and were allowed out only once every twenty-four hours. Meals were delivered by guards, the prisoners were constantly monitored, and security was ready to spring to action at the drop of a pin. Yet it was clear from the way he walked that Casso didn't feel safe.

Four state troopers stood at the far end of the wing, ready to escort Mel to the bus. The wing itself had twenty cells, the first ten of which were occupied by a motley assortment of women, none of whom were the least bit attractive to Groves. After that, the cells were empty.

"We keep Mel as far away from the other inmates as possible," Casso explained. "Mel has a…" He struggled for a word. "She has what you might call a bad influence on others."

"She makes them violent?" asked Eric.

"She makes them dead," said Groves. Three fatalities in this wing in the last month, with no cause of death determined. The only thing they had in common was being next to Mel Doe's cell.

Casso took out a handkerchief and dobbed his forehead. Not just out of nervousness; all the walking had taken its toll. "The cells are constantly monitored, and we went over all the footage. She never laid a hand on any of them. And yet..."

"And yet you believe she killed them?"

"It can't be coincidence."

Groves looked at the four officers standing guard outside the cell; three men, one woman, and not a sense of humor among them. They carried standard issue Glock 22s much like his own.

The female trooper caught his eye; corporal stripes, name tag T. Felice, not too tall, dark hair, nice shape. *Pair of thirty-eights and a real gun, too*, he thought. Not married, not in a relationship. He gave her a winning smile. Her eyes narrowed, just a little. Hard to blame her, this was hardly a social party. Maybe later at the airport.

Wait. *Pair of thirty-eights and*...this was her? This was her big entrance? A throw away sexist comment? She kept looking for a line from herself. "Felice said," "Corporal Felice frowned," even a mention of her first god-damned name! Nothing. She was just...there. One of four state troopers, the only one given any description whatsoever, and only because she had tits.

This had to be a mistake.

Eric chuckled something about Hannibal Lecter. "So did she get any of them to swallow their own tongue?"

Casso didn't share his amusement. "We don't have a proper C.O.D." That grabbed Eric's attention. "We had to mark them all as cardiac arrest, because nothing else fit. No sign of drugs in their systems, we went over both cells a dozen times. Nothing. But she killed them. I'm sure of it."

"The only thing I've killed is time, Warden."

The voice had come from the cell. Mel was dressed in prison orange. Her wrists and ankles were already shackled, joined by a long chain. Her red hair had been cropped short. She had a sweet smile, a coquettish tilt to her head, and a perfectly framed Garbo-like stare. But the eyes...

"The hell?" said Eric. The warden took a step back.

Mel Doe's eyes were entirely white.

"Hello, boys. Ready for the end of the world?"

Groves was amused.

"Nice trick. Too bad we're not in Vegas."

Mel's eyes rolled back down. It had been quite convincing; no strain on her facial muscles, no fluttering, no muscle twitch. If anything, she was more disturbing now that she had proper eyes.

"I'm limited in what kind of show I can put on right now, but I figured you were expecting something special."

Groves put his thumbs in his pockets. "That must have taken a lot of practice, or surgery. Part of your sermons?"

"Perhaps in the early days. I moved beyond that. But like I said, I'm limited in what kind of show I can put on right now. Give me time, hon. I don't disappoint. I've had tons of practice."

"I'm sure we all appreciate the effort." It was important to keep things light, not to let her think she had power over him like she did the warden. "I'd have you do my son's birthday party, but, well, you know. The whole 'evil' thing."

Mel gave one of her near-invisible smirks. "You don't have a son." She looked at Eric. "But he does."

Groves gave his partner credit; he didn't flinch. Groves's method of asserting control was to act glib. He had more comebacks than a stand-up at the Apollo. Eric took the more traditional route. "You understand why we're here today? We are here to escort you to the United States Penitentiary Administrative Maximum Facility in Colorado, where you will spend the remainder of your natural life."

Mel's demeanor changed completely. She sat

on the edge of her bed, one foot on the mattress, knee up, one on the floor. The chains rattled like they were for ornamentation rather than restraint.

"So get on with it. You're boring me."

Eric walked her through the procedure. Mel didn't listen. Her eyes were locked on Groves. That hidden smile grew just enough so no doubt lingered.

The smile said, *You and I are going to have so much fun.*

So that was it. Felice wasn't mentioned again in this scene. Presumably she had just stood the whole time in the background. Anger swelled. How dare...He? She? They? Who was she supposed to blame for this? What was she blaming them for? She was too angry to care.

She continued to read. She had to know what happened. More important, she had to see if she appeared again. She skipped ahead (a side story at a laboratory about a lady scientist going to watch a parade, the USS Carl Vinson in the South China Sea reporting missiles launched on Taiwan, the captain calling the President, blah blah blah). It wasn't until Exodus started that the story returned to Mel's cell.

The prison door opened and Mel Doe walked out, two of the state troopers in front, the other two in the back. She had to shuffle-jog just to keep up with their slow pace.

There was no trash talk from the other prisoners. If they felt anything, it was relief. She blew one a kiss and gave another a wink.

"See you soon."

She was taken to the yard where the bus was kept. The driver unlocked the rear door and she was secured inside the cage that took up the vehicle's back third. Two of the guards sat just outside the cage to watch her every move; the others sat closer to the driver. They weren't worried. They had dealt with some of the worst scum the state had to offer, usually in groups, and she was just one person.

No one noticed the hint of a smirk on Mel's

face.

She leaned toward the man closest to her. "So, handsome. Tell me about yourself."

Not even a reference to her boobs that time. Felice was as bland and faceless as the others. She didn't even know where she was in the bus. Was she sitting up front or in the rear? She didn't care about Mel or the end of the world anymore; she just wanted to know she existed. Somewhere. Anywhere. She wished she was reading this on a computer so she could use the search function, then imagined what it would do to her psyche if it came back with "1 Result Found."

She stopped to consider how little sense this made. She needed to find another reference to herself. Why? Validation? Did she exist *more* if this stupid book talked about her more?

None of that mattered. What mattered was knowing what happened to Fort Rock. What had this Mel person done, and how? Once she knew that she'd have a place to start, a reference point she could work from. She could find the flea. You can't know where you're going unless you know where you came from, right?

"That is one creepy bitch," said Eric.

"How much do you know about her?" asked Groves.

"Just the highlights. The CNN exposé on the cult. The standoff with the National Guard at their Oxbow compound and all that. I was watching when she surrendered and the whole building blew up behind her like she was in a god-damned Robert Rodriguez movie. That shit doesn't happen in real life, but there it was."

They returned to the parking lot and Eric took the driver's seat. He drummed his fingers on the wheel as they waited.

"How the hell did she know I had a son?"

Groves shrugged. "I knew, but it took me longer. She made a killing doing cold readings for séances before she started her church."

"All that crap she said about the end times. You know, when she surrendered? It was so Jim

Jones and David Koresh-like. But you know what the difference was?"

"You believed her."

Eric looked at Groves, unsure what had tipped him off. "Something like that. What was it she said at Oxbow? 'It would come to blows between the giants. But after the first, hell would be unleashed on earth.' You've seen the news."

Groves shook his head. "Typical evangelist bullshit. It could have applied to anything she wanted it to."

The front gates opened and the escorting police cruiser rolled out in front, followed by the bus. Eric waved to the driver and took up the rear.

To reach the highway, they had to drive downtown and hang a right at the main intersection. Eric kept three car lengths back, enough to clearly see the road ahead.

"The hell?"

A barricade blocked the street, forcing the caravan to detour down a side alley. A few blocks away, a parade was passing through; the muffled bass of drums and trumpets could be heard even in the car. A cement truck was slowly backing up.

"What the hell kind of parade does a nothing city like this need?" asked Eric. "Twenty-five years of running water?" He looked at a giant cartoon dog floating between the buildings. "I can't believe they can afford a balloon."

"Probably got it on sale," said Groves, who recognized the character. "That show hasn't been on the air since I was a kid."

"This is annoying," said Eric. He turned to follow the bus. Groves, however, looked more than annoyed.

"Why didn't the warden mention this? We should have taken a different route." Before they could follow the bus the cement truck had backed up and blocked the alley.

Eric slammed on the horn. "Back the fucking truck up!"

Groves got out of the car. He looked for the driver, but the cabin was empty. He drew his gun and tried circling the cement truck, but it was wedged in tight. He crawled underneath and saw the bus drift to stop. Only the top of the vehicle was still visible.

Groves yelled to Eric. "Drive around! Shit! They're breaking her out!" Once Groves cleared the truck, he got up and sprinted.

By the time he reached the bus, it was all over.

At the start of the next chapter, Agent Groves was examining the empty bus and dead troopers. But the answers she was looking for weren't in the book. Her death had happened off camera.

What was she talking about? Dead? She hadn't died. Somehow she had escaped and tried to leave town, but her car broke down outside this motel.

Not that anyone noticed, and that was just insulting.

Eric drove for ten minutes looking for Mel Doe. Nothing. He pulled up a few feet from the tire spikes, got out, and rolled the strip up. Groves was in the bus checking the bodies. The patrol car was still there, so Mel hadn't driven off.

"Any sign?" asked Groves.

"Nada. I called it in. The locals are getting organized." The radio in the car squawked. "That'll be them. Just a minute."

Of course they had to call the officials, organize a search, but something in Groves's gut told him it would do no good.Five men were dead, and there wasn't a single visible trace how. No gunshots, no ligature marks, no cuts, no bruises, not even a god damned runny nose. Four were found inside the bus; one lay on his back outside. The back door had been torn apart like tinfoil. And the part that made the least sense of all—it had been forced from the inside.

The idea that Mel had some way to kill people they couldn't detect was improbable, but like any magician's trick, it stopped being magic once it was understood. It was logical that she could still have followers who had planned to break her out, but the suggestion she had ripped open an armored bus from the inside without machinery? That defied reason.

Eric joined Groves at the bus. "That was Fort Rock PD. They're setting up a dragnet, but half the force is working the parade. There's some kind of panic going on down there. Fire broke out. Might be a riot. All kinds of traffic accidents. It's chaos, apparently."

That was hard to believe. While they could hear something going on, the surrounding alley buffered most of the sound. It didn't seem like chaos out there. Groves checked his watch. Just after eleven. "What did Collins have to say?"

Eric examined the bus for himself. "I couldn't get through to the Bureau."

"What? Why?"

"Don't know. Nothing is connecting. The police band in the car is working, though. Fort Rock P.D. is trying to reach them through landlines."

Groves muttered to himself. "And if that didn't work, they probably had a working telegraph office behind the old windmill." He stared at the empty cruiser. "Why didn't she take the police car? The keys are still in the ignition."

Eric stepped off the bus. "Hey, Groves, how many guards were supposed to be on board?"

Just then there was a bright flash that seemed to be everywhere. Their car engine died. The chatter on the radio was dead. In the new silence, the distant sounds of panic and confusion from the parade grew louder.

And he heard movement. Movement from

inside the empty bus. Too late, he saw a hand grab
Eric's ankle...

Felice closed the book and stepped outside, re-evaluating
everything she saw. The motel with its untouched and unlived-in
feel—everything in place but basic and generic, right down to the
big sign by the road that simply said MOTEL.

Like a child she stooped down and touched the asphalt. How
could she describe it? Hard. Bumpy. But was it real? She closed her
eyes. It was still warm from the setting sun.

The question wasn't *if* it was real. The question was what *kind*
of real it was.

She felt Mikey's hand on her shoulder. That was real, too. She
sat down and the boy joined her. She had recognized part of the
exchange between Groves and Eric. The puppet show.

"Is that why you didn't want to talk about your parents? You
don't know who they are and you're afraid you don't have any?"

He nodded.

"Is your name really Mikey?"

He shrugged.

"Did you find yourself mentioned in there? In the book?"

He nodded again. "In Exodus."

"What name did the book give you?"

"Boy."

"Boy?"

Mikey nodded and said in an even tone, "'The boy pulled at
the emergency escape handle as people with deformed hollow faces
poured into the bus, moaning and grabbing children into their final
embrace. As they reached the back seats, the latch came free and he
fell out, along with several others. They scattered into the crowd in
confusion, only to find the moaning horrors already among them.'"

How many times he had read that passage to have it memorized?
"That was you?"

The boy looked at his feet. "It doesn't sound so bad when you
read it."

Felice felt cold, and not just because they were losing daylight.
How different it must be to experience something so terrible, then
see it written. Written to entertain.

"Do you remember anything before this?"

Mikey said, "We were in a parade, waving out windows. Everyone was smiling. It didn't feel wrong. I was supposed to be there. Then I heard the voice." His jaw locked and he turned away.

Felice thought about the cryptic words of the doomed stock-broker. "*Her* voice? The tramp at the bowling alley?"

Mikey shrugged. "I didn't see her. I just heard a voice, really loud, like on speakers, so everyone could hear. Then I was all confused."

"Confused?"

"Before, it felt normal to be on a bus in a parade. That's all there was. Then I didn't know *why* I was in a parade, why I was waving, how I got on the bus. But I kinda knew *more,* too. I could tell everyone else was confused. And then..." He trailed off, paused, and flicked a small pebble on the ground.

"Then what happened?"

"Then the screaming started."

Mikey went back inside. Felice stayed outside and watched the shadows grow longer. There was a deep thump or rumble from the city. Felice turned her head and saw the tallest building in Fort Rock tilt, crumple, and fall sideways, sending clouds of dust high into the air.

She got up and went back to her room. Whatever.

Mikey was sitting on the bed. She dropped down next to him. Without making eye contact, the boy handed her a chocolate bar and a soda, one weary soldier to another.

She took them and looked at the labels. *Choco Bar* and *Cola* in large generic letters. *Well, at least they got the curly C right.* She snorted. She looked at the name on the television, which only said *Television* and didn't even have a logo. *A brand you can trust.* She chuckled. Mikey's school jacket lay in a heap on the bed. She picked it up and looked at the name on the crest. *Private School.* Its coat of arms was blank. *Worth every penny of its overblown tuition, no doubt.* She slipped into something between laughing and crying.

Mikey stared at the blank TV screen. "I know I like cartoons, but I don't know any." He looked at her with large, lost eyes. "I thought maybe we could make our own."

He raised his hand, now covered in a white sock with two black dots drawn on it in pen.

"Hello," the sock said in a high-pitched voice.

Felice smiled and wiped her eyes. She took off her shoes and pulled one of her black socks over her hand.

"Howdy."

"How ya doin?"

"Oh, aside from a major existential crisis I'm just fine and dandy."

The white sock tilted its head. "What's an egg-zin-sten-zil crisis?"

"It means I don't know who I am."

"You're a sock puppet."

The black sock nodded. "Oh, well, that clears that up."

"Hey, can I tell you a secret?"

"Sure."

Mikey's sock leaned in close to Felice's. "Your breath really stinks."

Felice's smelly sock attacked Mikey's face. The two laughed, and for a while their problems were forgotten. They played until it was time to sleep.

Felice wanted to tell him a story. She knew plenty of them, but every time she was about to start one she realized *that* story would be inappropriate under the circumstances. The Three Little Pigs? Little Red Riding Hood? Hansel and Gretel? Death and terror lurked around every corner, and there was enough of that outside their window.

The thought of *changing* the story to be more kid friendly, however, didn't sit well with her. Death was still there, just hiding deeper in the shadows, and that made it more dangerous. When it eventually found you, you weren't ready for it. You realize too late the blood and gore had been there all along, and your parents were just telling you what you wanted to hear. You were being *lied* to. And given their situation, this felt doubly dishonest, because she couldn't just lie their way to a happy ending.

Mikey was asleep long before she began to feel tired. Her mind buzzed with insanity—realities, contradictions, absurdities, impossibilities. She wanted to make some kind of sense of everything, but it all just swirled around her head in an endless loop. For a while she thought she'd never fall asleep.

Maybe she was trying too hard. Forcing things. What she needed to do was visualize the problem metaphorically. Let it come naturally. Walk herself through it. Maybe that way she could at least get some rest.

She pictured herself at a door—pretty convincingly, as it turned out. She could see herself from third person perspective in black emptiness, a door in front of her. For some reason, it was the green door to the hermit's bunker. She told herself behind that door was what happened to her that day. If she could open it, she'd remember everything. Except the door was locked. It needed a key.

The problem was there was no key hole. The hermit's door didn't even have a knob, just the eye slot. If there was no key hole, then there was no point in having a key.

But wait. The Gideon was the key, wasn't it? She looked down. It was already in her hand and fit perfectly into the eye slot. But the door still didn't open. She pushed and bashed against it, but what was the point? If she couldn't find a way to open it, it couldn't be opened. Maybe there was nothing to remember. Felice slumped against the door.

Just as she nodded off, the door opened, and she fell through.

DAY 0

Corporal T. Felice was on the prison bus. She was sitting at the front, watching the road. She looked back. Mel was still talking to the guards. She didn't know why; the prisoner had never talked to them before. Said they were boring.

At a detour, the driver hung a tight right. One of guards by the cage leaned and fell over. When the bus straightened out the guard on the opposite side fell over as well. They didn't move.

Felice looked at her partner who had gotten up to check on them. Up ahead, the patrol car stopped. The trooper waved them down, pointing to a tire spike strip ahead of them.

She called to the driver. "Something's wrong!" The statement applied equally well outside and inside.

The driver pulled to a stop. He checked the rearview mirror, opened the door, got the first aid kit from the overhead compartment and ran back to the other guards.

Felice moved to join them, but something stopped her. Mel hadn't reacted to the scene at all. If anything, there was a faint smile on her lips. Mel asked the guard and driver something, but Felice couldn't hear what. Why were they answering her? She looked past Mel out the rear window. The FBI escort was nowhere to be seen; only a cement truck blocking the alley. Then she looked back at Mel.

Her eyes were gone.

This wasn't the eye trick she'd pulled in her cell. They weren't white. They weren't even black. *They weren't there at all.* Sockets like open mouths gaped and the two men slumped onto the others in a heap. Mel cackled as though Felice wore silver slippers—or was that ruby?

This was the point where she should have rushed to help her comrades. Where she should have drawn her weapon. Where she should have given Mel some ineffectual command to stop whatever the hell she was doing. Where she should have put a bullet between her hollow bloodless sockets.

Because a bullet would *totally* work on someone who was laughing at you without any fucking eyes and who managed to pile up four bodies without lifting a finger.

Felice grabbed the shotgun from the driver's seat and jumped out of the bus.

She felt a tug at her shoulder, as though the void from those eyes had reached out to drag her back in, but she pushed through.

She crashed into the officer from the escort car, stumbled, hit the ground and rolled. There was a rending sound of metal from the back of the bus. She got back up and ran, jumping over the tire spike strip at the end of the alley. The other trooper called after her, but was cut off mid-sentence.

Felice didn't look back.

She kept running.

There was no thought behind this, only instinct and timing. A survival impulse at the root of her brain stem overruled everything outside of breathing. Behind her was death. Not a possibility or probability: a certainty.

The world had become a distorted tunnel, blurs on all sides, ears full of white noise. All that mattered was what was straight ahead. Legs screaming, lungs burning, it didn't matter. Only when her muscles threatened to take her down did she finally give in. She turned a corner and braced her back against a brick wall, hoping to avoid that empty gaze. She held her shotgun up to her chest, gulping air like she was drowning.

The seconds passed. Her breathing slowed. She needed help. She checked her radio, but it was gone. It must have come off in the tumble.

Dammit. Why didn't I try to stop Mel Doe?

Because you'd be dead then, too.

One bullet could have ended it.

That wasn't going to work.

How do you know? Wait. Am I talking to myself?

You see anyone else willing to give you the time of day?

That was a valid point. The streets were deserted. Of course the parade would be popular—God knew there was little enough to do out here—but the whole town? Not even a drunk asleep by a dumpster?

So now what?

Trust your instincts, they got you this far.

Then what?

Sorry kid, you're on your own.

Swell.

Another survival instinct kicked in. People. The parade. Now that her ears weren't filled with her own rushing blood, she heard the din of laughter and cheers and high school bands. She had to get to the parade. People meant safety. Other police officers. Help.

She peeked around the corner for any sign of Mel. Nothing. She gauged the direction of the parade and began to jog. Her legs had put a moratorium on running.

A few blocks later, she saw the back of the parade. Felice breathed a sigh of relief. The closer she got the more people she could make out, there was even a big dog balloon hanging over the crowd at the rear. She saw two police cars at the rear. *Thank God.*

She heard a woman's voice call out over loudspeakers, but she was too far away to make out what was said. Then the dog balloon began to rise, and some cries of excitement came from the crowd.

Wait. Not excitement. As the balloon went up, she saw someone was still hanging on to the one of the ropes. At first Felice thought it was a child, but it was a woman, blonde with a ponytail. Why didn't she let go? She should have known better than to hang on. But that wasn't the only strange thing going on. The crowd was behaving oddly. It was no longer a party.

It was a panic.

The police cars Felice had seen were rocking back and forth. One was suddenly turned on its side. People scattered in all directions. The mob was attacking the police. She saw four drag a trooper to the ground; his partner backed up, weapon drawn and shouting, not knowing whether to fire or not, only to get pounced from behind by three others. One of the police cars caught on fire.

Her first thought was this was some kind of riot, but they weren't just attacking the police. They were attacking each other. Screams of terror mixed with screams of pain and madness.

In the last fifteen minutes, the world had gone insane; men and women tore at each other like rabid animals, embraced like crazed lovers, smashed store windows with their bare hands, or staggered on fire swinging at everything around them. The cruiser exploded, knocking some people down and setting others ablaze. Half the city was on a rampage, the other half was trying to escape. For a moment, it seemed those evangelist bastards who ranted about the end times had been right after all.

Felice stood on the street with her shotgun, frozen to the ground as the orange and black plume of flame from the cruiser climbed skyward, blotting out even the balloon that still drifted with its struggling stowaway.

A second cruiser drove toward her, trying to get away from the carnage, but was covered by three crazy people. Two had arms inside the car through the half open door, manhandling the driver. They dragged him out, the car lost control and spun, everyone fell into broken heaps on the pavement. Two got up; close enough for her to see the whites of their eyes—if they had had any.

That snapped Felice out of her trance. She raised the shotgun and fired, knocking the man down flat. Instead of blood, gray ash burst from his chest. A dozen others who hadn't noticed her before now looked—if they could look—in her direction.

Felice ran for the car, shooting the second crazy who had gotten up point blank, kicking a spray of ash twenty feet behind. There was no hope for the trooper dragged from the car; his skull had cracked open in the fall, staining the asphalt red. She got in the car, engine still running, as the mob rushed her.

Shit shit shit shit shit!

She floored it and drove off, leaving behind a cloud of burnt rubber. One or two neurons took the time to ask what the hell those things were, the rest focused on keeping the gas pedal down and not crashing. She needed to get out. Out. Out of the parade, out of the city, out of the *state*.

The good news was there were no hoards of crazy eyeless people in front of her. The bad news was just about everyone who could get to a car was also driving out of town and panicking more than she was. By the time she reached the main street, she was in the middle of a demolition derby.

An SUV clipped a Smart car, which hit a hydrant and rolled like a golf ball into a house. A red Camaro whipped past Felice with the top down. The passenger, a blonde woman who had been slumped over, suddenly lunged at the driver and sent the car careening into a

Dodge van, which fell on its side and blocked the road. An old station wagon smashed into her side, attempting to evade the oncoming wreck. Felice barely managed to avoid the ensuing pileup, going wide off road, running over a speed limit sign and almost losing control in the dirt before clawing her way back to the asphalt. In the rear view mirror, she saw fire and smoke. No one else seemed to make it around. If anything, the pileup grew wider.

The blinders came back and Felice sped away from the city. She only snapped out of it when a bright flash of light filled the sky and the engine stalled, causing the cruiser to drift slowly to a stop on the shoulder of the road.

Felice calmed down. She looked at the gas gauge. It wasn't empty, so why wasn't she moving? She tried the engine again, but got nothing. She got out and took in her surroundings. Far behind her was the city, sitting on the plains like an oasis or an island. Smoke rose from the east side. To her right: nothing but parched grassland as far as the eye could see. To the left, a single level motel, and beyond that were mountains with dark clouds forming behind them.

She checked her watch: 11:02. It wasn't even noon, but she needed to rest. Just a little rest. Just enough to calm down, get her head together.

She took the shotgun from the passenger seat and headed for the manager's office.

DAY 4

Felice awoke with a gasp. For a moment, she thought it was Day 1 and she would re-live the last three days all over again. Mikey groaned and rolled onto his side of the bed, reminding her where and when she was.

"Is that how it happened?" she asked herself. She hadn't actually expected the visualization exercise to work; she was just trying to get some sleep.

The events had appeared to her haphazardly at first, jumping from image to image, then stretched from scene to scene, and finally came together like a jigsaw puzzle, where it took on a kind of hyper reality—as if she'd been editing it together on a computer, then was sucked into the screen.

Maybe she made it all up.

She was struck with a half-conscious inspiration. What if that didn't happen, but *could have* happened? Maybe the only thing missing was putting it on paper. If this was a story, maybe she could write it. Re-write it. Take it over. Could it be that simple?

There was just enough light to see by in the early morning twilight. Felice put on a fresh shirt and went outside, taking the notepad, bible, and a pen with her. She didn't want to wake Mikey just to have him grind the flashlight for her.

She ripped out the pages she'd already used, stuffed them in her pocket, and began to write. She filled in that page and the next with what she remembered of the dream, taking care to be as accurate as possible. Then she summed up the events she remembered until today, including what she'd found in the Gideon.

When finished, she looked at her words. She wrote surprisingly neat, even when rushed. She waited. After a moment, she realized she didn't know what she was waiting for. Had she expected the words to glow and disappear or something? Probably not.

She opened the Gideon and scanned for changes. None. She searched for the story boundary. It had advanced two pages since last night, with Agent Groves getting lectured by Doc McKay for destroying a whole building. But Felice's words weren't there, or anywhere before that.

She sighed. It had been a long shot anyway.

Felice was cold. Not wanting to wake up Mikey, she walked around the parking lot, thinking and rubbing her arms. Had her objectives changed? Not really. She was fond of living and fond of Mikey, so survival was still the number one priority.

Maybe the hermit lady was right. Maybe they should just stay put and ride this thing out. They weren't important. Nothing would come after them unless they attracted their attention, right? Right. Except...

...the end will come all the same...

Felice wondered if the hermit knew what was going on. When she thought about the old woman's words, particularly her "history" lecture, it seemed possible. What had she said? Something about a general and three trusted soldiers going into battle? Getting inside a fortress somewhere to find a healer? It might have just been Felice's imagination, looking for patterns where none existed, but it sure sounded like the hermit had been talking about Groves and his men leaving to rescue the doctor from the prison hospital.

The horizon to the east had turned purplish-red, the city of Fort Rock now visible to the north as shadows.

Felice tried to take everything she knew up till now and create a hypothesis. She thought about the details of the town, and the generic look and feel of the motel. She opened the bible again and turned to the first page. It started at chapter three. What happened to one and two?

She went to the manager's office and picked up a couple of keys. She checked the nightstands of those rooms for their Gideons and brought them out into the light.

They were all missing the introduction and first page. They all started at chapter three. They all told the same story.

So her book wasn't unique. She didn't know if that was comforting or disturbing. She filed this information away for later. For now, she focused on the opening of chapter three where Groves and his partner first arrived. After reading it a few times, she nodded and went to the patrol car, still parked in the middle of the road. She got the spare tire out of the trunk and walked down to the Fort Rock city limits sign.

She rolled the tire down the middle of the road, away from the city. It rolled, slowed and fell over. She walked up to it and did it again. And again. And again. And again. By the fifth roll, the tire started becoming indistinct. Once it stopped rolling, it was hard to tell if it was a tire or not. It was just a black blob with a silver blob in it.

She remembered when she first met Mikey—if she hadn't stopped him he'd have kept on walking until he was nothing at all. And what if her car hadn't zonked out next to the motel? She shuddered.

This new break in reality didn't faze Felice for long, however. You got used to them after a while.

Satisfied, she returned to the motel. Just as the sun broke over the horizon, she saw the city limits sign welcome her back:

NOW ENTERING
FORT ROCK CITY LIMITS
POPULATION 500

Felice blinked. Okay, *that* caught her off guard. The numbers hadn't fallen off or been painted over. It just said *500,* as if it always had. She distinctly remembered it said 4000 before, and hadn't the first paragraph of the Gideon said 20,000? Reality was keeping score.

"That *can't* be good."

Felice talked to herself all the way back to the motel. She knew it was the crazy cat lady thing to do, but even crazy cat ladies were saner than this place.

"Point one: this is a story. The story takes place in Fort Rock. Nothing really exists outside city limits. Therefore there is no escape. At least not for most of us. That's because of...

"Point two: Agent Groves is the *hero* of the story. The story follows him, so he should be able to escape, along with anyone with him. Unfortunately that brings up...

"Point three." She glanced back at the population sign. "Everyone else is expendable."

With the sun now sitting on the horizon like a golden basketball she moved on to things she didn't have answers for.

"Question one: How do we survive the story?" The answer to that had to lay in understanding the story.

"Question two: All stories are about something, what is the story about?" She assumed it had to do with the villain and her motivations.

"Question three: Who is Mel? Is she just another character, acting out a role, or is there more?" Felice walked back into her room, having forgotten the notepad in the parking lot.

She picked up the radio/flashlight and started to crank. The DJ should be starting his programming day soon. Her timing was excellent. *Good Day Sunshine* played for a while, then the DJ's voice cut in.

"Good Day, Sunshine. Good day, *everyone*. You're listening to What The Hell Happened radio. We're still accepting submissions for a better station name, but that means you have to find a way to contact me. I'll be giving the frequencies we monitor in a few minutes, but first, let's get any new listeners up to date. You've probably got all kinds of questions. I'm sorry to say I don't have many answers."

"I might have a few," said Felice.

Mikey woke up and Felice got him to wash, eat, and get ready as soon as possible. The radio hadn't been much help today. Most of what was said they already knew, but at least they were still on the air. She prepared the backpack for a possible two-day trip. They wouldn't take the wagon this time; she had other plans.

"Grab your Harley, kid. We've got a busy day ahead of us."

Before they left, she took the T. Felice tag off her dirty uniform and put it in the upper pocket of the clean black shirt she'd put on. She felt she had to keep it. It was the only connection she had to any kind of identity, really.

She picked up the notepad from the parking lot as they left, along with one of the Gideons. It was hard to think of it as a bible anymore, but it was, perhaps, the most important piece of survival equipment she had.

They made good time back to the city. Felice was so focused on getting things done she barely noticed the weight on her back. Mikey, too, seemed unusually determined. They passed the pile up and headed straight for the hermit lady's bunker.

Within a hundred yards of the building Felice knew something was wrong. As they got closer, 'wrong' got a 'horribly' tacked in front of it. The front of the store had several unburned bodies scattered about. The door had been forced open. Felice's shoulders tightened, but she didn't panic. If anything she became more focused.

"Stay here," said Felice. She loaded the shotgun. "If something bad happens, ride back to the motel as fast as you can." Without an adult, Mikey's fate could be worse than whatever might happen in the store, but what choice did she have? She wasn't about to give a nine-year-old a crash course in firearms training.

"I'll be very careful," she said, for her sake as much as his.

Felice approached the door as her instincts told her to: back against the wall, crouch, then ease the door open with her shoulder, shotgun leveled. Once inside, she checked the blind spots. The store was a mess. The lights were on, but several sections of track lighting had been smashed, and a couple flickered. Clothing racks had been knocked over, buckshot and bullet holes were in every wall, dust and bodies lay scattered on the floor, all with the same grim visage. Despite her misgivings, it was probably safer for Mikey to be here with her than wait outside. She waved him in.

"Don't look at them, Mikey," she said. "Stay by the door and keep an eye open for me. Scream if you see anything move."

"I'm not a girl!"

Felice smiled. "Then use your whistle. Or give me a big manly yell. Go 'Argh!'"

She searched for the hermit, but it was too much to hope she was still alive. She hadn't gone down easy, though. Behind the counter, in a puddle of brass and plastic casings, were two pistols, a pump shotgun, and an assault rifle Felice bet had been converted to full auto fire. A pile of clothes sat next to the guns, but no body. Odd.

From this angle, she realized most of the toppled clothing stands were in a straight line, as though someone had run through them. Aside from the bullet holes, a deep crack split the rear wall, like an earthquake had tried to rip the place in half. Straight above the missing body was a hole in the ceiling. Sunlight came through in a shaft, landing a few feet from Mikey.

She almost said "The hell?" but stopped herself. She'd said that a lot lately. More had happened here than just getting overrun by Moaners. Her gaze fell back to the hermit's clothes. Why were they in a pile next to her weapons? Had she jumped up through the ceiling like Superman, so fast her clothes had come off? Did some kind of satellite laser beam vaporize her, magically leaving her clothes intact? Was she still alive, running around in the open plains buck naked?

The latter seemed the most disturbing possibility.

"I'm sorry I wasn't here to help," said Felice. She glanced back at the carnage in the store. "At least you gave them a hell of a fight."

She pulled out the Gideon and checked what she had missed since leaving the motel. Maybe the answer was in there.

She read aloud. "Blah blah blah, Groves argues with the Doc. Blah blah blah, she thinks there's a scientific explanation for everything. Yeah, right. Blah blah blah, Groves fights off Moaner attack. Blah blah blah, brings more people to Haven..." Nope. Nothing. Whatever happened here had been off-camera, so to speak.

Seeing as there had been no tweets or manly "*Argh*"s yet, she assumed they were okay for the moment. She tossed Mikey a chocolate bar and picked up some extra boxes of ammo—slugs, buckshot, pistol—as well extra clips for the Glock. Looking around, she realized she could arm herself to the teeth, but what would be the point? It hadn't done the hermit lady any good in the end.

She searched under the counter for anything useful. The first thing she saw was a tin box which looked fifty years old, covered in knobs, switches, and some kind of display with a needle on it. Next to the device was what looked like an upright shower head resting on a thick book.

It took her a moment to realize she was looking at a CB radio. Granted, she had one back in her patrol car, but it was new and something about this model positively reeked antiquity—the kind of antique that was nearly indestructible. Whatever happened here had left a dent in the front of the machine and cracked the glass display, but the power was still on.

Felice checked on Mikey before picking up the microphone and setting it on the counter. She turned up the volume and squeezed the handset.

"Hello?"

There was a hiss of static, but no reply.

"Anyone out there?"

More static. Then a woman's voice. "Ten-four. Is there a ten-thirty-three at Miss Cleo's?"

She understood all the words, but what she heard made no sense. "What?"

"Is everything okay at Miss Cleo's, four-ten?"

She assumed the hermit was Miss Cleo. The words sounded like trucker lingo. She didn't recognize what she heard, but did know a few radio terms.

"Um, negative. We have a two-forty-six and multiple four-ninteens here."

"Can you repeat that? Didn't copy. Come back."

Felice shook her head. It was almost funny. "Never mind." They knew completely different radio codes.

The woman on the radio asked, "What's your twenty? Are you the bear past checkpoint Charlie?"

Felice vaguely remembered that bear meant cop in trucker lingo. Checkpoint Charlie probably referred to the big pile up barricading the road. She had intended to drop her police identity now that she wasn't wearing a uniform, but it seemed more convenient to stick with it for the time being.

"My name is Corporal Felice and I'm with the Oregon State Police. I've been staying at a motel outside of town."

"Full grown bear, ten-four. What can I do for you?"

"Well, we can start by not throwing numbers around."

"Roger that."

"Who is this?"

"My handle's Yuri. Where are you?"

Felice recognized the name as the person working with DJ on the radio. "I'm at a camping goods store not far from the pile up on the south side of town." Felice surveyed the wreckage. "What's left of it. An old woman used to live here. She's gone now."

"What happened?"

"Looks like a major firefight. Moaner bodies everywhere. Even the roof's caved in." She didn't bother mentioning the pile of clothes next to her. Too weird to explain.

Silence on the radio for a moment, then, "Damn."

"Did you call her Miss Cleo before? Like the psychic?"

Another pause. "Yeah. She was our eyes and ears out there. Warned us about things before they happened. She also talked kind of cryptic-like."

"I noticed." Felice looked at the clothes and restrained herself from the obvious should-have-seen-it-coming psychic joke.

"It's going to be a lot harder for us without her there. You interested in taking over?"

"Can't. I've got a kid out here. Need to get him to Haven ASAP.

Can you give us directions?"

"Negative. Not a secure channel. Only Agent Groves can give that information."

"Where's Groves now?"

"Not a secure channel. Keep an eye out for a red flag."

No new information there. Felice sighed. This was the only sane adult contact she'd had. And while comforting, it made her feel more isolated than ever. "How...how are things out there?"

"You mean Moaner activity? Pretty quiet. It's like they're waiting for something."

"No. I mean...with you. How are you holding up, Yuri?"

Another pause on the radio. "You make the most of what you have, when you have it. I've got DJ during the day, and the stars at night to keep me company. It's beautiful, you know?"

"Stars? World's going to hell and you're looking at stars?"

"Have you seen them? There's no power anywhere. You can see them all. You can see the Milky Way. Sit still long enough and you can almost feel our little ball of rock rolling slowly through the cosmos. Our world's going to hell, sure, but there are billions and billions of others out there that must be doing okay for themselves. There's some comfort in that. So, what about you? What keeps you going?"

Felice looked over at Mikey, who was picking his nose. "Duty."

"That's it? Not terribly romantic, are you?"

Felice smiled as Mikey sniffed his finger. "Depends on how you look at it."

Yuri said, "Well, Corporal Felice, I've got another band of survivors holed up out there waiting for a chance to find Haven. Keep an eye out for them, would you? Maybe you can help each other."

"Will do."

"We have to move our set up now. I'll be out of contact for an hour or so. Hopefully I'll see you at Haven soon."

"Hopefully. Thanks."

"I'm gone."

Felice put the microphone back. The book it had been resting on was a battered leather bound copy of the *Decline and Fall of the Roman Empire*. She picked it up and flipped through the pages. The first two chapters were missing, but aside from that, it looked like an ordinary history book—nothing that seemed to be about Fort Rock. Her memories of Miss Cleo's sermon must have just been a coincidence.

When she put the book back, she noticed a button under the cash register, presumably for a silent alarm. Felice stifled a laugh and pushed it. Maybe the police would come.

Instead, a buzzing sound came from under her feet. She stepped aside. The button had unlocked a floor panel, which she pulled up. Underneath was a floor safe. It had been broken into already...or perhaps it simply hadn't been locked. She lifted the heavy lid and found only ashes inside. Money? Who would burn a safe full of money?

She sifted through the ashes. Not everything had burned. Toward the bottom, she found hand-written pages, charred, but some parts still legible. She picked out several fragments.

> "...we've got Fifth and Rockafeller blocked off, sir," the policeman said over the car radio. "But we can't be sure they won't find another way around. Hell, they could be on the..."
>
> ...no circumstances was Vimy to remain in the hands of the Huns. Blast and damnation, didn't H.Q. realize what the real terror was they faced here? At least the Huns were...
>
> ...passengers on the locomotive screamed as it crashed off the bridge, taking with it the only way off this god-forsaken island. "Heaven preserve us," said Lady Truss. "That was..."
>
> ...as the queen strode through the courtyard. She ordered her musketeers to hold the line, no matter the cost, lest these horrors breach the inner sanctum and...
>
> ...she came to the festival full of wonder and desire. The city of Görlitzhafen was so alive, so full of—

Felice's heart skipped a beat. Déjà vu all over again. Görlitzhafen? Why did that name sound familiar? Wait. Festival. She'd dreamed about a festival in a medieval town almost every night. She'd just assumed her pre-amnesia self had been really into Renaissance fairs.

> ...she came to the festival full of wonder and desire. The city of Görlitzhafen was so alive, so

full of life and opportunity; she knew she had to
have it. She wanted everything the city had to offer.
Everything...

The passage sounded so familiar, yet alien. Like she knew exactly what the fragment was talking about, but hadn't actually been there. No, that didn't sound right, either. She strained at the thought, grasping at cobwebs, but came up blank.

She looked back at the fragments, trying to find a pattern. They were written in the same hand, but weren't from the same story. *Fifth and Rockafeller* implied one was in New York. *Vimy* and *Huns* suggested the First World War in Europe. The one with the locomotive might have been from the same era, but it sounded earlier. More Victorian. The queen and her musketeers had to be at least a century before that. And Görlitzhafen...

Why were these here? What were they about? Why were they burned?

She shook her head, no time for this now. She pulled every legible scrap from the safe, placing them between the early pages of the Gideon. She'd deal with this later.

Felice caught Mikey staring into space. "Good job, kid. Nobody snuck up on us." She took a couple more chocolate bars and tossed one to him. "Time to go."

"Where are we going?" It was the most probing question the boy had asked to date.

"Exploring," said Felice. She patted the Gideon. "We're in search of the wild and elusive protagonist."

Felice had a plan. You can't stop a tidal wave, but you *can* ride it to shore—just so long as you didn't get smashed on the rocks or dragged back to sea. If she and Mikey were insignificant and expendable extras in an end-of-days story, then the key to survival lay in becoming central to the plot.

It was far from a guarantee—in fact, it could backfire completely—but it was better than the alternative. Besides, while everyone knew they were insignificant in the grand scheme of things, it was somehow worse to see it demonstrated on paper.

Step one was tracking down Agent Groves. Unfortunately, the Gideon never gave the exact location of Haven; otherwise she would have just shown up on their doorstep with Mikey. As it was, they had to work for their grand entrance.

The re-write of the Gideon had progressed as far as Lamentations. How appropriate. The Doc had sent Groves and his volunteers to pick up some equipment vital for making a weapon she believed could stop the Moaners en-mass.

What Groves didn't know was Terry, the only person to survive the bowling alley firefight after Groves and the Doc escaped, had been taken by Mel herself (in an unnecessarily erotic fashion). He was now living on borrowed time as a mole, with Mel whispering inside his head.

After returning to Haven, Terry had briefly lost his grip on normality, and sucked the life out of a new survivor. When he regained his composure, he hid the body, then 'discovered' it along with Groves and shot the corpse as it began to reanimate. All the while, Mel laughed in his mind.

Felice didn't understand how all that worked, but rolled with it. Everyone else was.

It wasn't hard tracking down Agent Groves now. At this point, the Gideon described his team following the old parade route, where the outbreak first spread. Felice remembered the area well enough to get there in good time. Mikey kept up on his pink bicycle. She referred to the book every couple blocks, using the red ribbon bookmark to track the narrative event horizon.

The Gideon worked in a curious way; despite the fact the

Moaner story was formatted in chapters and verses like the bible, there were differences. With the exception of Genesis, none of the books had chapters, they were chapters unto themselves. The font was slightly different—Times New Roman versus Lucerna. The size was different—twelve point as opposed to ten. The former used left justification while the latter used full.

This made it easy to spot the boundary and see how the story had crept along, yet it never happened while the book was open. Nor was the creep consistent. Hours could pass without a word, then a page would fill in less than ten minutes. Sometimes the words along the boundary changed. The meaning was always the same, but the current paragraph was always in a state of flux, with words being dropped or added every time you looked at it.

She checked the Gideon again but found nothing useful. Ahead, she saw a yellow school bus, its back door wide open. Mikey looked uncomfortable. He had ditched the bicycle a block or so behind and was walking beside her. She allowed it because the street was too cluttered with the debris of the initial panic to make biking practical, but Felice knew he just didn't want survivors to see him riding it.

"Is that the bus?" Felice asked. "Your bus?"

Mikey nodded. The words *Private School Bus* were printed in black along its side. It was empty now, as was the whole parade route aside from a few ashen bodies. Everyone had fled or been infected (Converted? Morphed? What did you call the process?)

She hadn't heard any gunshots or anything else to indicate something was happening. In the story, it seemed to be smooth sailing for Groves's crew, which probably meant they were well ahead of her. Felice and the boy moved along the parade route, past a float celebrating a local sports hero and one honoring the city's something-something anniversary. The tattered banner wasn't terribly clear on this point.

She kept checking the book for an update on Groves's progress, hoping for a reference point she could zero in on. When she reached an overturned dairy float, she found it.

"There." She pointed to the page. "Keep an eye out for the Lutz Institute."

It just so happened the Lutz building was clearly marked with large metal letters over its entrance. Inside the vestibule, she saw movement.

Fighting the eerie feeling this overlapping of realities gave her,

Felice began phase two. No longer dressed as a state trooper, she'd decided the best way to work her way into the narrative was to adopt a new persona.

She burst inside the front glass doors, Gideon in her right hand, shotgun raised like the staff of Moses in the other.

"Halt, sinners!" was the best she could come up with. Groves and his men spun around, weapons at the ready.

They were, to say the least, confused.

"You seek an end to the blight, but I am here to say that it is *here* among you!" Her gaze locked onto Terry. "One of you possesses the dark taint of *evil* and will *betray* you before you find it!"

Agent Groves was easy to spot. FBI jacket aside, he was the best looking of the bunch. Strong jaw, perfect light brown hair, and smoldering eyes that right now were rolling upward. "We don't have time for this, lady." He looked to Mikey next to her. "Jesus Christ, did you bring a child into a hot zone?"

Terry walked over to Felice. "You want me to take them back to Haven, boss?"

"Yeah, do that. We'll be all right." Groves and his men turned to leave.

Okay, this wasn't going according to plan.

Terry held out his hand. "Why don't you let me hold that weapon for you, ma'am?" he said in a patronizing tone. "I'll get you somewhere safe."

Felice's mind raced to find the best way out of this. Only one option came to mind—violently.

She dropped the Gideon and kicked Terry in the crotch, then knocked him onto his back and stepped on his chest, shotgun aimed at his face. Groves and the others trained their weapons on her.

"Drop the gun!" yelled Groves.

Felice ignored him. "I don't have time for this bullshit, Terry. So why don't you just tell your buddies how you *really* escaped from the bowling alley, huh?"

Terry stammered, "I have no idea—"

"Drop the gun *now!*" said Groves.

Felice stared at the prone man. "Who are you going to kill next time for a few more hours of life?" Terry's eyes widened. "You're a ticking time bomb and you know it."

Agent Groves had given her some kind of ultimatum, but Felice wasn't really paying attention. It was just her and Terry now. She could tell he knew the truth, or perhaps a different version of it. He was a pawn and wanted a way out, just like she did. Only there wasn't one.

She leaned closer so only Terry could hear her. "I know she's in there. What's she saying?"

Terry's expression betrayed his surprise and confusion. "She wants to know who you are."

"That makes two of us. Terry, you want to make things right, don't you? How the world remembers you will be defined by your last act."

Groves was giving her a count of three to stand down.

Terry almost laughed. "*What* world?" But she knew she'd gotten through. "I'm sorry, guys!" he said, leaning up. "I never wanted to—" He never finished his confession. His body shook, his face contorted and his eyes sunk into a void within his head. His body fell back, and lay still.

Felice backed up, lowered her gun and gave the FBI agent plenty of space. Groves waved his men to stay put. He walked over and looked at Terry's empty sockets. Felice leaned in look as well. A tiny black void seemed to be swirling inside, getting larger. Groves raised his rifle and shot Terry once in the chest, which burst into ash. The void faded.

Groves paced toward his men, stopped halfway, then back to Felice. "What's your deal?" he asked. "Psychic? Agent of God? Lucky guess? Spy? Bear in mind those aren't in order of what I consider most likely."

Felice considered her answers as she picked up the Gideon. "I've come to help. I think I've proven that, and I think that's all that matters." After all, in a novel nobody just blurted out their whole back-story and motivations up front. There had to be a reason to come back to the character, things to reveal later. Things Felice would have to make up.

Groves looked her over, then the boy, then nodded. "Stay here. Guard the entrance. We'll pick you up on the way out, get you some place safe."

Felice agreed, and Agent Groves took his men up the fire escape stairs. The door shut and Felice nearly collapsed in relief. She went down on one knee and took a deep breath.

"Are you okay?" asked Mikey.

"The question is, are *we* okay?" She opened the Gideon and found nearly a page had been filled regarding their big entrance.

"Not bad. I sound pretty cool. A bit crazy, but cool."

Mikey tried to read over her shoulder. "Am I cool, too?"

"Sorry, kid. Looks like I got the limelight. You'll be cool later."

"I *am* cool," he insisted, showing off his Better Dead Than Red t-shirt.

She found the verse where Terry confessed, and the scene played out through Groves's eyes, more or less.

> The woman backed up, lowering her gun. Groves signaled the others to cover him as he examined Terry's body. He looked at the woman. How did she know? She talked like a preacher and carried a bible, but...he shook the thought out of his head.
>
> Groves put a round into Terry's heart; a rose of ash burst from his chest. Another man lost. First Eric, then the twins, the first convoy, then his team at the bowling alley. And just when he thought fate had smiled on him and one had gotten out alive, it turned and kicked him while he was down.
>
> He approached the newcomer. "So what's your deal?" he asked her pragmatically. "Psychic? Agent of the Lord? Lucky guess? Spy? Keep in mind those aren't in order of what I consider most likely."

Interesting. She distinctly remembered him saying 'God' not 'the Lord.' And how the heck did you ask something pragmatically?

> The woman picked up her bible. "I've come to help. I think I've proven that, and I think that's all that matters."
>
> Groves looked her over. Maybe she was crazy. Maybe she wasn't. He didn't have time to deal with this, but she had a kid with her. He nodded. "Stay here. Guard the entrance. We'll pick you up on the way out, get you someplace safe."

It had only gotten as far as them in the fire escape stairwell. Presumably nothing would happen until they reached the floor they needed. Felice looked around the vestibule. "Might as well get comfortable."

They went behind the security desk and each took a chair.

"Are we safe here?" asked Mikey.

Felice shrugged. "More or less. We have a good view at least. I'm guessing Groves's men have more to worry about than we do." She searched the desk drawers. "All right!" She pulled out a deck of cards. "So, what's your game, kiddo? Texas Hold 'Em or Go Fish?"

Twenty hands of Go Fish later, Felice heard faint echoes of gunfire.

"What's that?" asked Mikey.

She checked the Gideon. "Looks like Groves and company are on their way back. The top five floors had been sealed off by lab staff trying to survive the outbreak, but one had been infected. Groves had to break in to get something called an electromagnetic resonator and they all got loose. Ooops. Now they're sliding down the elevator cables to escape. It's all very exciting."

The gunshots got louder, and loud thuds hit the ground floor elevator.

She closed the Gideon. "Guess we're leaving." She got up and grabbed her gear.

Mikey looked worried. "Is this a good idea?"

"It's gotta be better than staying at the motel, right?"

"But there's not as many bad things out there."

Felice understood how he felt, but she couldn't bring herself to tell the boy the motel was on the edge of limbo. Maybe it made sense to be out there, but it felt like living on borrowed time. Haven had to be a better place for Mikey.

A few more blasts, then the elevator doors began to pry open. The car was wedged halfway between floors with Groves and his men on top. Felice came over and gave them a hand.

"Thanks." Groves hopped down. "Let's go. Bring the kid. Next stop, Haven."

As they stepped outside, one of the men took a red flag from his jacket pocket and tied it to his rifle. The width of the flag had been fitted with a collapsible antenna so it would stay unfurled and not droop. The standard bearer held the rifle so it rested against his shoulder with the flag in full view. From a distance, they must have looked like a bunch of children, playing war.

As they took an unfamiliar path through Fort Rock, Groves said, "I don't know if you've been listening to our radio broadcasts, ma'am, but that flag is so survivors know we can take them to safety."

"So I've heard," said Felice.

"We might pick up a straggler or two on the way."

"God works in mysterious ways." It sounded like the right thing to say.

Groves cocked an eyebrow so perfectly it had to be his signature expression. "Sure. Look, lady, about what happened back there. Care to fill me in? Or did 'God' speak to you?"

She hadn't really thought this part through. She should have worked out her whole back-story at the motel instead of running on gut instinct, but it was too late now. At this point it was better to stall and see how things developed. "You're not a believer?"

Again, it seemed like the thing to say.

Groves pointed at a body. It lay on its side on a bus stop bench; hollow drooping eyes, no endless void. You could see the back of its head, a sign she took to mean it was really dead. "I don't recall being told about any of this in Sunday school, Preacher."

Preacher. Good, that was a distinctive moniker. "I'm not at all surprised. But it does say the dead will rise in the end of days."

Well, she was pretty sure it did.

"Yeah, well, I'm not about to settle in and wait for the four horsemen to drop by, thank you very much."

Felice smiled. "Neither am I."

"I can see that." He stared at her, even more puzzled. "You don't strike me as a preacher, you know."

She forgot Groves was supposed to be keenly observant. But there was a problem with that — they had met before. It was the only reason she had part of a name. Why didn't he recognize her? She tried not to appear nervous. "Looks can be deceiving. You of all people should have learned that by now."

Agent Groves considered this. "Guess you're right. I've been off my game ever since my partner...I mean, I knew Terry was acting strange, but I thought it was post-traumatic stress." He frowned, as if looking back for the signs he missed. "So what about the boy?

What's his story? Those aren't his regular clothes."

She saw no need to lie about Mikey, and told his story more or less straight.

"And you've been holed up in a motel all this time?"

"Mostly. We've made short trips to the city outskirts once we heard your radio broadcasts. Picking up supplies, looking for red flags." She chose not to mention the hermit lady, since Miss Cleo was tied in to things she'd rather not talk about. "Tell me about Haven. Sounds lovely."

Groves shrugged. "It's just a secure location. Easily defended, heavily provisioned. Lots of space. It's not Shangri-la. DJ thought the name would make survivors more likely to come out."

"DJ? You mean on the radio?" she asked. "Is his name really DJ?"

"It's just what I call him, Preacher. Simplifies things. He and his gal run the transmitter from the roofs of some of the buildings. She's been in contact with some other survivors, hidden in other locations, giving us most of our intel."

Felice sensed a possible complication in the future if Yuri figured out who she actually was. She'd cross that bridge when she came to it.

"Was the flag his idea, too?"

"No, mine."

They seemed to be working their way to the northern edge of the city. It was the farthest Felice had been from the motel, which, up till now, had been her own idea of Haven.

"So what do you know of this plague?" she asked. Anything was better than thinking about how uncertain the future was.

"Not sure I'd call it a plague, Preacher. Not sure *what* I'd call it. It's not natural. I don't know if the Doc's science or your religion can explain it, really."

Felice clutched the Gideon to her chest. "Guess it depends how you define either of them."

They reached a large building, the only one over eight stories before you left town, and turned down a ramp to the parking garage. It had both a steel shutter and a roll down barred gate protecting it. On one side, a small hole had been cut; Felice saw an eye looking out.

"You vouch for 'em, G-man?"

"Always do."

"The quarantine's twelve hours now."

Groves said, "Twelve? It was six."

"Doc's orders. After you and Terry found that guy dead inside, the Doc extended it."

Groves frowned. "I'll talk to the Doc. I have a feeling that was a one-shot deal."

The eye looked left and right. "Where *is* Terry?"

"Different kind of one-shot deal."

Felice shook her head as the two gates opened. How many lines like that did Groves have on an average day?

Over a dozen armed men were just inside the gate. One was assembling a rifle, others played poker, but seemed ready to jump up at a moment's notice; the rest stood or sat in various states of preparedness. On the opposite side of the peephole was a guy at a makeshift desk of monitors—some color, some black and white. They had power; lights ran down into the garage.

Groves touched the shoulder of a man tinkering with all kinds of electronics. They surrounded him in a big convoluted pile like a nest. "Still nothing on the cell phones?"

"Nothing."

Groves didn't seem surprised. He pointed out the CCTV setup to Felice. "We cobbled that from a bunch of home security cameras we got from Home Depot. We have coverage two blocks in every direction. Took a day to put that together. Further than that and we have lookouts with binoculars and walkie-talkies checking in. Better than how we started, when the survivors were still an unorganized mob. We try to track Moaner movements so people listening on the radio know when it's safe to come out. The internet goes down and suddenly a radio feels like a caveman banging two rocks together. Can you believe it?"

"W-T-H-H indeed," said Felice.

Groves snorted. "I suggested G-T-F-O as a station name, but DJ's choice was more appropriate. I was still in panic mode then."

Felice looked at the man. The way he walked, the way he talked, the way he, well, did anything. "You don't look like the panicking sort."

"I'm not. I like to be ready for any situation. But this? Come on. Don't tell me it didn't catch you with your panties around your ankles."

Felice tried not to roll her eyes. "Are you like this with all the ladies?"

"Just the ones I like."

"Right, the dipping pigtails in inkwells school of charm."

Groves shrugged. "Works for me."

Felice wanted to say, *I bet it does,* but instead asked where quarantine was.

The FBI agent pointed to a fire door next to a city bus covered in metal plates. "That stairwell only goes up one floor. We barricaded the stairs above that so no one can get in or out. I'm sure I can get the Doc to let you out in six hours. Maybe less if this do-hickey she's putting together works."

Two men stood by the fire door.

"Anyone still in there?" Groves asked.

"Two guys, a woman and a kid. Been eight hours. They were ready to leave when the quarantine was extended. They ain't happy."

Mikey pulled on Felice's arm and said, "No shovel."

"There's a little porta-john in there," said the guard. "But...yeah. That's about the size of it."

Felice looked at Agent Groves. "Try to make it less than six hours. Please."

❧❧

Inside the stairwell, friendly introductions were offset by various chemical and organic smells competing for dominance. A man wearing a leather vest and American flag bandana on his head paced on the upper landing. "It's plain as day I'm not one of *them*. Why bother?" It appeared to be his favorite, if not only, talking point.

"Why didn't you just ride your Harley out of here?" asked Felice.

"What makes you think I ride a hog?"

She looked at the *Born to Ride* tattoo on the man's arm. "I'm a world class detective in my spare time."

"Well, those things tore up my ride."

The woman of the group shook her head. "Wouldn't have mattered. The roads were blocked."

"Which ones?"

"All of them," said her husband—Felice saw the rings. "We tried four different roads out of the city. Three had pile ups, one had the bridge out. All of them had those *things* waiting on either side. I didn't want to drive off road and risk them swarming the car."

Felice thought about the truck that had crashed into the motel restaurant. "Probably the right choice." But why hadn't she been attacked at the pile up? Maybe that had been the last of them, or the rest wandered back to town?

All this time, Mikey had been studying the child in the group. A blond kid Mikey's age, wearing the same non-descript school uniform Mikey had on before. Felice didn't know what was going on there. They never said a word, only stared at each other.

"We found him hiding in an alley," said the woman. "He hasn't said much."

"Shock," said her husband. "That's all."

That wasn't all.

"So what's your story, Preacher?" asked the biker. "Going around telling everyone 'I told you so?'"

"This isn't His doing, if that's what you're suggesting."

Depending on who you meant by *Him,* of course. Felice's thoughts began to wander on the subject.

"Whatever, lady. I'm just here to grab a gun and shoot at anything that moans."

A moment passed before Felice realized the biker had unintentionally set up a joke. She blurted out, "That's what *she* said." Judging from their unimpressed expressions, it hadn't been the best time to try and lighten the mood. "You know...the gun is his penis," she added. "Shooting... moaning..." She thrust her hips in a final bid to make her point.

"I don't think that makes sense," said the husband. "Aren't you saying *she* said she's here to grab a gun and shoot at anything that moans? Are you talking about a transvestite?"

"Timing was off," added the wife. "It felt awkward and forced."

"Don't quit your day job, Preacher," said the biker.

≈≈

An hour later, they were back in the garage. A guard took the others deeper into Haven, while Groves talked to Felice.

"Quarantine's lifted. After I explained about Terry, she reassessed the data. No one exposed to a direct Moaner attack has survived more than an hour."

"What about another like Terry?" asked Felice. "He lasted a good day."

"Doc thinks he was on some kind of borderline between alive and whatever...whatever crock of bull she calls them. Unique case rather than a mutation."

"He was being used, you know. By *her.*"

Groves looked at Felice sideways. "Don't know what you're talking about."

"She's at the heart of all this, isn't she?"

Groves's face gave away nothing. "Still no clue."

Felice didn't know how to play this. He knew all about Mel. Was he keeping her out because he didn't trust her? Perhaps there were things he didn't really know, but a reader would have pieced together. She chose to press the issue.

"Look, I know who—"

Groves cut her off. "Listen. There's what you know and what I know, and then there's what everyone else knows. Think carefully before you go blabbing about *her.* People have enough to worry about here without us adding to it."

She had considered shoving the Gideon in his face, if only to show him up. *You think you have problems now, mister FBI man?* But she thought better of it. What would the ramifications be? For all she knew, it would cause some kind of meta-antimeta collision and the world would implode on itself. She didn't feel like risking it.

Groves took her and Mikey down the next level; a barrier had been erected at the top of the ramp, made of cars and sheet metal. One car was pushed aside a few feet to let them pass.

"Second line of defense," said Groves. "In case we're breached."

The parking lot beyond was full of furniture and other household items, grouped together and organized within several adjacent parking spots each, giving the impression of an apartment building floor with the walls removed. Over a hundred people milled around like it was just another day.

"We brought the furniture down before sealing the stairwells and elevator shafts," said Groves. "This garage has three floors. The next one down is like this, too."

"Where are the cars?"

"It's an unfinished building; it was never full to begin with. Those that were here were protected from— " He stopped himself, then continued. "Most tried to get out of town, but that never seems to end well. Not individually. We're organizing a mass exodus, but we've got nearly four hundred men, women and children down here, and only two buses."

"There was a school bus on the parade route."

Groves nodded. "So I heard. We're picking that up later, but it still leaves us a bus short, even with the SUV and a couple of other cars we got working. I've got some ideas, though." He looked like he was trying to convince himself. "Make yourself at home. Come find me if you want to help out." He nodded, a bit more wearily than she expected, and left.

Felice waited a moment, then turned the Gideon to find the new boundary.

> "...but that still leaves us one bus short. Don't worry, I've got some ideas. Make yourself at home. Come find me if you want to help out." He gave the Preacher a confident grin...

Talk about an unreliable narrator.

Felice and Mikey found an empty space near the back and borrowed some chairs and a coffee table from a family that had stuff to spare. They'd mingle later, but for now it just felt good to be somewhere by themselves, even if the walls were invisible.

"Was that boy one of the kids you escaped with?"

Mikey nodded.

"Do you know him?"

Mikey shook his head.

"You stared at him pretty intently."

"I thought I *should* know him."

"Did he know you?"

Another shake. "Maybe I don't have friends." Felice could understand the self-pitying sentiment, but then the boy surprised her. "Maybe nobody does. No friends. No moms. No dads. Just them."

It struck her just how lonely these people must feel. They focused on the threat at hand to avoid thinking about how little they knew about their own lives, if they thought about that at all. Better to live in the moment. She remembered the notepad in her backpack.

"Maybe they do." She pulled it out, along with a pen. "I had a dream the other night about what happened to me before. Some of it, anyway. So I wrote it down, thinking it might make it really real. Let's do that for them."

She pointed to the man across from them. "That's Chad, he gave us the table. Who do you think his parents are? Let's give them names."

Without hesitation Mikey said, "Mary and John."

Felice wrote down:

> Chad was a middle aged man with thinning
> hair and a slight paunch. His parents, Mary and
> John, always told him...

"What did they tell him?"

"To eat his vegetables!"

> ...to eat his vegetables and be nice to strang-
> ers, which is why he gave Felice and Mikey his
> coffee table.

Mikey smiled, and she knew why. He liked how that fit in with what actually happened. Felice knew Chad wouldn't suddenly remember the names of his parents or to eat his vegetables, but it was a kind of magic nonetheless. In Mikey's mind, Chad was less lonely now, which made Mikey less lonely.

"What about her?" Felice pointed to a woman sitting by herself. "You think she has a boyfriend who's looking for her?" Mikey nodded and Felice started to write.

They played these character developing mad-libs until just about everyone on the floor had some kind of back story. Caught up in the moment, she rubbed Mikey's hair. "What about you, kiddo? Let's get you some parents."

Mikey's smile fell. He slowly shook his head. "I don't have parents."

"Everyone has parents. You just don't remember them."

He shook his head again. "I don't know them because they don't exist."

"You don't know that. They could be here in Haven waiting for you."

"They don't *exist*." He was getting angry now. Mikey understood the situation better than she realized.

Felice tried to calm him down. "There are couples here. Couples who know they must have children but can't for the life of them remember who they are, what they look like. Maybe you could be that child." Mikey shook his head. "Don't you want a mom and dad?"

Mikey nodded, and looked at her with big brown eyes.

The implication struck her like a thunderbolt. "Oh. But I'm not—" She indicated the lack of a gold ring on her finger. "And I'm pretty sure I never—" She waved at her belly, gesticulating the messy business of birth, like she had grown a watermelon in her hands and spilled it on the floor. His eyes stayed locked on hers, as if wishing hard enough would make it happen. His body language was universally understood.

Please?

Felice turned the page.

> Corporal Felice had adopted little Mikey two years earlier, after her sister died in an accident. Working long hours at the prison to pay for the private school he attended, she never got to know the boy as much as she'd wanted to.

She stopped a moment to look Mikey.

> If one good thing had come out of this nightmare, it was the fact that this had finally changed.

Mikey read what she had written and hugged her. After letting it sink in for a moment, she hugged him back.

Mikey was asleep on his chair, covered by a thin blanket. Felice couldn't blame him; it had been a hell of a day. She watched him breathe—her son breathe. That had a nice ring to it. *Her son.* It sounded utterly alien to her, but nice. It also made her even more resolved to keep him safe.

She had told him the story of Hansel and Gretel before he fell asleep, scary bits and all. If anything, she tried to make the scary bits *really* scary. It seemed counterproductive at first glance, but Felice had had what she considered an epiphany. She wasn't protecting him by not telling him these stories, she was leaving him unprepared. Without the fear, the message didn't get through. Yes, the world was a scary place full of danger. But if you were clever and alert, you could survive. You could *win.*

She got up, grabbed her Gideon, and looked for Agent Groves.

It didn't take a genius to tell if this was a story, it was the kind that ended with very few survivors. If she and Mikey were to be among them, there were only a few options open.

She found Groves on the top garage level, the staging grounds, going over a map of the city with some more men he'd recruited. With them was someone who didn't quite fit in with the others—sun burnt, hair like a wheat bale, jeans, and a white t-shirt with *W-T-H-H?* written in black marker.

"I'm sorry, it's too late," said Groves. "You know we can't send anyone."

"After everything she's done for you?" Felice recognized the voice; this had to be DJ. The wild-haired man looked like he wanted to punch someone, though the size of his arms indicated this would have little effect. "You can't just leave her!"

Two of Groves's men seemed ready to carry him out, but the agent waved them to stop and shook his head.

"What happened?" asked Felice. "Leave who?"

Groves gave her a 'not now' glare, but said nothing.

DJ turned to her for support. "You know our radio?" He puffed up his tiny chest showing the broadcast letters.

"Only station I listen to."

"Groves won't let us broadcast from this building because we think, you know, the *bitch* might figure out where we are."

"Mel," said Felice. Groves gave her a look that warned her from saying too much in the open.

DJ seemed to know the score. He lowered his voice. "Yeah. *Her.* She's the reason we don't tell people where Haven is. Moaners probably don't listen to radio, but *she* might. We broadcast from the lower rooftops. Well, we did."

Felice's heart sank. It just occurred to her who was missing. "Wait. Is this about Yuri? Did something happen to her?"

Groves raised an eyebrow. "You know her?"

"We spoke once, over the radio. A couple hours before I found you." Felice realized in the pit of her stomach that she was composing another brief eulogy. "She seemed nice."

"Don't say it as if she's dead!" DJ yelled. "She's missing! Look, we always chose locations that couldn't be reached from the outside. You know, fire escapes and the like. We were *always* secure."

"So what happened?" Felice asked.

"We'd just moved to a new building, and I was going back for our camping gear."

"Camping gear?"

"They stayed on the roof to guard the equipment," said Groves. He clearly didn't approve of the practice.

"I was coming back up the stairs when I heard a scream and..." It took a moment for DJ to compose himself. "All I found was some of her clothes, a gun, and this." He clutched a book by Carl Sagan. "We have to find her."

Something about the scenario didn't add up. "Are you sure there wasn't another way up to the roof?" asked Felice. DJ thought about it, then shook his head. Felice frowned. "So why didn't they get you first? How did they get to her at all?"

DJ was ready to explode. "*I don't know*, but she's out there somewhere. We have to find her!"

"You think she jumped off the roof of a building and is running around town naked?" Felice pictured her skipping with the hermit somewhere in the grasslands.

"All I know is I can't find Yuri and nobody's helping me!"

"I'm sorry," said Groves. "We can't do anything now. You know we can't. She's gone. Get some rest. We have to think about the others."

Something in Groves's voice seemed to get through to DJ, even if he didn't want to accept it. He grumbled and left, still clutching the book. Groves sagged. Felice got the feeling when anyone had a crisis, he was the one they went to. It was taking its toll.

"I never understood why they insisted on staying up there," said Groves.

"She was into astronomy," said Felice. "You can see the Milky Way out there now."

"Still seems foolish to me."

"You make the most of what you have, when you have it." Felice repeated Yuri's words without really thinking, then snapped out of it. "We all have our ways of staying sane, I guess."

"I guess. It would explain DJ. He used to be a lawyer, but he volunteered to work the radio. Said it was something he always wanted to do."

Felice pictured the weedy man in the shabby clothes and wild hair in a courtroom. "A lawyer?"

"I know, he doesn't look it."

"Guess that goes for a lot of people here."

"True," said Groves. "Can I help you, Preacher?"

"Just wondering if you have a minute."

Groves dismissed the others. "We're done. What's on your mind?"

"Can we speak somewhere private?"

Groves pointed to an unoccupied corner of the garage. Felice tried to lighten her voice as they walked over. "I never got a chance to thank you."

"As I recall, you saved *our* lives."

"Yes, but you brought us here. You brought my son here."

Groves stopped in his tracks. "Your *son?*"

"I'm not Catholic, Agent Groves. Ever heard of a female Catholic priest?"

"Oh. Of course." They continued on. "Divorced?"

"I adopted him when my sister died." Might as well keep the story straight.

"Well, I was happy to help. This last week has been hell. Every time I get someone to Haven, I consider it a victory, and they treat me like a hero. But they don't know about the others. The ones who ran. The ones who were caught. The ones that fell behind." Groves's eyes grew distant. For all the bad things she'd seen, he must have seen ten times worse. The spotlight was on him, after all. For a moment, she reconsidered her plan.

Groves saw the look on her face and smiled. "We do what we have to, Preacher. We help who we can."

Felice nodded. *That* she could understand. "You're a good man, Agent Groves. You have a noble way of looking at things. Don't treat it like a burden. It's your strength." She stopped and took a step closer to him. Now came the hard part. "I hope you don't think I'm being too forward, but it's been a long time since I met anyone like you. It's usually the broken men, the downtrodden, the criminals, those that need to be shown the light. But you—" She tried to keep herself from gagging. "—you *are* the light."

She couldn't help it—she gagged. That speech had sounded better in her head. She couldn't believe she was doing this. She turned the sound into a sob and leaned on his shoulder. "I'm sorry. I'm no good at this sort of thing. I mean, you're a handsome FBI agent, you probably already have a girlfriend and I'm just..." She let the words hang, hoping he'd fill in the pause.

"Hey, don't put yourself down. You're a good woman. You saved your son, you saved my life and, well, you're beautiful. When you burst in on us at the Lutz Institute, I thought you were either a nutjob or some kind of avenging angel. I'm glad it was the latter."

Felice didn't have to fake her blush. Groves *did* have a way with his words. Maybe it was her proximity to him now, but something about him was genuinely attractive, even seductive. He had the carefree charm of a James Bond type of hero.

She brought her lips to his and they kissed. She dropped the Gideon and wrapped her arms around him. His lips were powerful, electric; she felt like the center of the universe. She didn't want to let him go.

When she opened her eyes at last, she saw a man that was everything she ever wanted. "I guess there's no place *really* private around here?" she asked.

Groves nodded his head to a stairwell. "That one doesn't have a chemical toilet."

"I'm there."

"I'll join you in five minutes. Have to take care of something first."

Felice picked up the Gideon. She was almost dizzy and felt lucky she made it to the stairwell without falling over. Inside, she felt her heart race as she waited for him. She undid the top three buttons of her shirt to expose enough of her bra to be alluring. She wanted to relive those last five intoxicating minutes. She smiled when she realized she could, and opened the book.

> "...When you burst in on us at the Lutz Institute, I thought you were either a nutjob or some kind of avenging angel. I'm glad it was the latter." *More or less*, he added to himself.
>
> The Preacher blushed and looked at him with longing. She was beautiful, but looked like she hadn't been kissed since she joined the church. She threw herself at him and clumsily locked her lips on his. For a moment, Groves thought about Doc McKay, but that was going nowhere and the Preacher was right here. He kissed her back.
>
> "I guess there's no place really private around here?" she asked.

She kept reading as the warm feeling inside her quickly turned cold. Groves was trading jibes with the men in the supply room, congratulating him on "getting some."

> "She may be half crazy, but the other half is all kinds of hot," said Bill.
>
> The others laughed and two of them fist-bumped.
>
> "Knock it off, guys," said Groves. He picked up a bottle of wine and two plastic cups from a crate. "We're tired and lonely as hell down here. If we can find just a little bit of happiness, we shouldn't make light of it. Life's too short. That said," he added with a smirk. "No interruptions for the next two hours. *Hooah!*"

Felice slammed the book shut. Unreliable narrator or not, it couldn't be that far from the truth. She was pissed. Groves was already interested in someone, and was going to use her because she was *convenient?*

But for all the anger she had for Groves she knew most of it should be directed right back at her. How was she any better? At least Groves hadn't tried manipulating her, which was more than she could say about one T. Felice, regardless of good intentions. She'd been prostituting herself. His only crime was taking advantage of the opportunity she'd given him.

Still, what an *ass*.

Just then Groves opened the door, wine in one hand and cups in the other. She kneed him in the crotch. "Don't worry, I won't interrupt you for at least two hours!" she yelled as she marched back down to her invisible room.

The encounter had drained her; she wanted nothing more than to forget the whole thing as quickly as possible. Within ten minutes of collapsing in her chair next to Mikey, she was asleep.

Felice was in a field. The sun was directly overhead, which should only ever happen if you lived south of Texas. The grass beneath her feet wasn't just dry, it was dead. When she brushed against the blades, they broke and turned to ash. There was no buzz of insects, not even a breeze.

Miles away to her left was Fort Rock, a tiny concrete collection of broken building blocks. Far on the right, she saw the back of the motel, which was so low and flat it only stood out because of the sign next to it. She could just make out the arrow from here, as well as the squad car nearby.

And behind her, much closer than they had ever been before, were the mountains. The dark clouds roiled and green heat lightning flashed behind them, as if the storm those peaks contained was just waiting for the chance to spill over and engulf the world.

She looked back. There had been movement. Something from the motel. Something waved. An arm. A person. She couldn't make him out at this distance. He was just person-shaped. He tried to get her attention, walking toward her, waving both arms. Then he lowered his hands to his face.

Areyouthere?

Felice barely heard the word, which seemed to have drifted over in its own lazy time, but there had been no other noises to drown it out.

Felice looked toward Fort Rock. There was another figure approaching. This one didn't wave.

Even at this distance, she could make out the black clothes and red hair.

DAY 5

All too soon (though perhaps not soon enough, given how her dream was going), Mikey woke Felice up to ask if he could play with the other kid from the private school. Felice had written down that his name was Jeremy and he and Mikey were best friends. Now Mikey wanted to convince the boy of it.

Felice started to wonder what had compelled him to ask permission. No one had ever taught him to behave that way. Was it instinct? Convention? Felice stopped herself. If she went down that road, she wouldn't see Mikey as a real person anymore—then she wouldn't be far behind. She'd wind up mad in a field watching grass turn to dust and asking existential questions until the storm rolled over her.

She ripped out the page about Jeremy and gave it to Mikey, who hugged her and ran off.

When Felice looked back at the notebook, she found herself staring at a single word written halfway down the page, written by a hand that was not her own.

Hello?

In a normal world, the word didn't have to mean anything. In a world where the dead didn't suck the life out of people like morbid vacuum cleaners and current events weren't recorded in the bible as they happened, it wouldn't have. It could have just been someone testing their pen on a random page some time back. But this wasn't that world. This was the other one—the one where those words had to mean something.

She turned the page.

Areyouthere?

She almost heard the voice from across the field.

She'd stared at the page as if deciding between the red and blue wires of a bomb. What was this? How should she respond?

First thing first—eliminate the possibility it was some kind of coincidence. Easier said than done, but she went with her gut and wrote at the top of the page:

Hello. Who are you?

She waited, but nothing appeared. She shut the book, counted to ten, and opened it to the same page. Still nothing. She looked at the page behind it.

Help me.

She flipped through all the pages underneath. They were still blank.

Felice was stirred out of her trance by a deep rumbling voice. It was a big man, Toby, the member of Agent Groves's team that had used his sniper rifle as a flagpole. She was pretty sure he'd just said something to her, but for the life of her didn't know what.

"Sorry?"

"I said Doc McKay wants to see you. Next floor down. In the back with all the lights and doo-dads."

Felice looked back at the page where she'd just had the strangest five minutes of her life—and given the last week, that was saying a lot.

"I'll...I'll be right down."

She soon found herself walking deeper into the parking garage, clutching the notepad and Gideon to her chest like protective wards. She didn't really remember getting up in the first place.

Some residential space had been set aside for survivors on the bottom floor, but the back half had been reserved for a different kind of work. A generator hummed in the corner, and a number of long collapsible tables had been set up in a half-circle near the back wall. The tables were covered in laptops, books, mechanical parts, coils, and any number of devices she couldn't begin to describe. The one that stood out most looked suspiciously like a 1950s death ray, polished to the point where she could see her reflection. The half moon display on its side showed the weapon to be fully charged.

A woman with long blonde hair was working with a microscope next to a computer. "Just a second." She jotted down some notes then looked up. She looked more like a model than a scientist, right down to her pouty lips and flawless skin. She put on her glasses. Something about the woman seemed strangely familiar. She had been at the bowling alley, of course, but—

Then it clicked. The woman had been dangling from the parade balloon during the initial outbreak, she remembered how she looked from the dream. Did that mean it really happened that way? And how the heck did she survive that? Felice must have skipped that part of the story. For an end-of-the-world drama, it had a lot of filler.

"Ah, hello." The woman shook Felice's hand. "We haven't been introduced. I'm Doctor Catherine McKay, but I'm sure you'll just call me Doc like everyone else. You must be the preacher David found."

Felice frowned. "David? You mean Agent Groves?"

"Of course." The Doc blushed. "I'm sorry, last night he brought down a bottle of wine and—but that's neither here nor there."

Felice rolled her eyes. That was quick. "What an *ass,*" she muttered.

"Pardon?"

"He sure has class."

Why was Felice surprised? Looking back, it was obvious Doc McKay would be Agent Groves's love interest. All the bickering she'd read in the Gideon pretty much made it a certainty. If Felice had accomplished anything at all, it was just to get them together sooner. She had to rethink her strategy. At best, her role in this story was going to be Fifth Business, but perhaps that was enough for her and Mikey to make it.

Doc McKay adjusted her glasses. "Agent Groves tells me you have some special insight regarding the Moaners, as everyone seems to insist on calling them. I was hoping you could share what you know with me. Anything at all would be useful."

Felice nodded. "Sure, but I don't know what I can tell you. My insight, as you put it, is more behavioral, predicting their movements. It's not like I have enough warning to be useful."

"You were useful in spotting Terry as compromised."

"That's different. I had an inside track, if you follow me." She knew the Doc wouldn't, but that wasn't Felice's problem.

McKay's eyes narrowed a bit. "God? You don't exactly talk like that kind of preacher."

Felice tried not to stammer. "I have my moments. I'm more

of a street preacher, you might say. Worked with the inmates at the penitentiary."

The Doc's gaze grew distant. "Those poor people."

"What do you mean?"

"I'm sorry, I suppose you haven't heard. I was at the penitentiary not too long ago. I needed to get Patient Zero's medical records and samples from the infirmary. She went back there after the initial outbreak. I saw what she had done there. She'd gathered them, somehow. It was like she was building something and using them as...those poor people."

Another chapter she must have skipped. Probably better if it stayed that way.

Felice considered telling the Doc the truth about the situation, but decided against it for the same reasons she hadn't told Groves. Still, she could tell her what she learned from the Gideon's version of events; it had been rich in overblown exposition on this point.

"Okay, Doc. Patient Zero, as you called her, was the leader of a death cult that was into all kinds of dark magic, trying to bring about the end of the world, and ninety-nine percent of it was baloney. But something did take. Before she surrendered something got inside her—a demon perhaps—something that gave her the power to drain the life from others, turning them into husks of their former selves, who then do the same to others, trying in vain to fill the void within them. They have faint echoes of their memories and nothing more. All the power in the city somehow got knocked out after she escaped. This city is, for all intents and purposes, isolated, a hundred miles from nowhere in every direction. That's good news as far as the rest of the world is concerned, but for us it means we're screwed."

Felice took a deep breath, having said it all in one go. It sounded like nonsense, she knew, but it was the explanation the Gideon gave, and if you couldn't trust the bible, what could you trust? Felice waited for the Doc's reaction.

"Cute."

"Excuse me?"

Doc McKay pushed her glasses onto the bridge of her nose. "Well, you're a good observer and I credit you with doing your research. At least you don't think it's some kind of Chinese bio-weapon like most of the others here, or embellish details the way Agent Groves does. Well, aside from the demon reference." She paused a moment. "I'm sorry. I don't mean to be disrespectful. It's just that talking about black magic, essences and demons won't help us stop this. This is unlike anything you've ever seen, I know, but I assure you there is a scientific explanation to the outbreak."

Did she really *expect* Felice to talk about this scientifically? "Dammit Doc, I'm a preacher, not a scientist."

The Doc still seemed disappointed. "I know. I just hoped you might have had something useful for me."

Felice wanted to smack the blonde out of her. "Well, why don't you enlighten me, Doc?"

"I'm afraid you wouldn't understand."

"Use small words."

Doc McKay went over to a dry-erase board. "Very well. Mel Doe, or 'Patient Zero,' had millions in financing through her 'religion,' and while on the surface she did practice 'black magic,' this was just a means of maintaining psychological control over the 'faithful.' Standard cult practices." Air quotes shot through the garage like suppressive fire.

Doc started scribbling equations and diagrams on the board. "What she was really interested in is called Quantum Resonance Organic Compression, something we've been researching at the Lutz Institute for over two decades, ever since the Manhattan Lockdown back in '88. Mel had dozens of scientists on her payroll pursuing this in a lab underneath her compound. We know this because some of them used to work for us."

Felice's left eyebrow inched upward.

"A quantum computer can out-process anything we currently use. Instead of using bits of data, it uses qubits, and functions in many more states than the traditional two, thus exponentially increasing processing power. QROC stipulates organic matter might be able to function in a similar fashion. If the human brain could, in effect, be made into a quantum computer, our understanding of the world would increase exponentially. 'In apprehension, how like a god!' to quote the Bard." She continued to draw on the board.

"I believe Zero's team made some kind of breakthrough, but at a price. The quantum compression manifested as a singularity of sorts. Unstable, and needing to absorb matter in order to keep from evaporating like a black hole. That's why a dead Moaner's head is just hollow, while a living specimen seems to have a void—the latter has a working compression field."

The Doc went on like this for ten minutes, drawing diagrams of the human brain and how it could maintain synaptic and nervous connections in a QROC state, how the field could pass from one person to another, how it desiccated the body in such an unusual way, and why the singularity only focused on the brain. When she finished, Felice nodded.

Then she burst out laughing.

Doc McKay wasn't expecting this. "What's so funny?"

Felice kept laughing, pointing at the whiteboard. She tried to stop but couldn't.

"Stop it!" said the Doc. "You're being ridiculous."

Felice gasped for air. Her sides hurt.

McKay scowled. "Really now, what seems more reasonable to you: black magic and zombies, or that this—" She circled the diagrams on the board. "—is all a QROC?"

Felice had almost recovered, but that sent her over the edge into another fit of laughter. "You think..." she managed between breaths. "You think all that makes sense, don't you?"

"I don't expect *you* to understand, but *I* am a scientist!"

"Oh, I know. The glasses, lab coat and ponytail are a dead giveaway."

"Stop mocking me!"

Felice wiped a tear from her eye. "I'm sorry. I'm sorry. I'll be good. It's just..." If she tried to explain, she'd only crack up again. She pointed to the strange shiny weapon on the table. "Okay. What about this? What does this do?"

Doc McKay sat down and started working on her laptop. "I don't see why I should bother telling you anything."

Felice tried to control herself and act serious. "Look, I may not understand the, er, *science* but I know we're facing a serious threat. Agent Groves told me you were on the cusp of creating a weapon that could stop the Moaners in large groups. Is this it?"

Doc McKay sighed and waved to the device like a bored showroom girl. "That is a weaponized electromagnetic resonator. If it works it will destabilize the QROC field in a wide—" Felice was already starting to snicker. "I've had it with you. Get out!"

Felice took out her notepad and started writing. "No, wait, let me get this down first. This is gold!"

"SECURITY!"

Toby had been watching from a distance but seemed reluctant to interfere. Eventually he sauntered over and escorted Felice away as she continued to scribble notes.

She didn't know why she'd laughed so hard. Obviously, everything Doc McKay had said was gibberish, but that shouldn't have been enough. Perhaps after everything she'd been through something had to give. At this point, two humping dogs would have sent her into hysterics, and woe betide anyone if she got her hands on a cream pie. She felt positively *goofy*.

Back in her 'room,' Mikey waited, playing with the other private school boy. The two were taking turns building a house of cards. It wasn't like they had Legos.

"Guess what! Guess what!" Mikey said, almost knocking the house over. "I remember something!"

"You mean, from before?"

Mikey nodded. "Uh huh! A really real memory! Jerry has it, too!"

The other boy nodded.

"Jerry, huh?"

"He didn't like Jeremy. Jerry's close, right?"

"Sure is." She wondered if this memory was just part of a game, but played along. "What do you remember?"

"Just before the parade, we were all at the library. We were looking at the books there, and they showed us the new bookmobile!"

"It was big and green and looked like a caterpillar," said Jerry.

"And they told us they used it to send books to the small towns far away that don't have libraries of their own."

"They keep it in the fire department garage!"

They were so excited about remembering something before all hell broke loose—even by just a few hours—that Felice felt a little jealous. She didn't have any memories like that. She was conceived in foreshadowing, came to term in tension, born in terror, and lived in a world where a QROC was a sound scientific theory. "That's wonderful. You didn't make that story up?"

They shook their heads. Jerry said, "Nope! When we started hanging out we just kinda remembered."

Felice moved to find a seat.

"Careful," said Mikey. She had gotten a little too close to their house of cards.

"Don't worry. I'm just going to read a bit." Felice tiptoed to a chair and sat down.

She looked over what she had written at McKay's lab, trying not to laugh all over again. It wasn't easy, especially since she had written "HAHAHA!!!" next to some of the more memorable bits of gibberish. She was no scientist, but neither was McKay. That was for damn sure.

Felice felt like a child holding onto a big secret—she was dying to tell someone. Mikey knew, of course, but how much did he really comprehend? She didn't want to bake his brain discussing metaphysical philosophy with him. He was too young to wear a beret and start smoking French cigarettes, anyway.

She turned the page, hoping to organize her thoughts.

Not my strong point.

Felice froze. She'd forgotten about the notebook. As before, the words had appeared on the next page, not the one she had written on. Was it referring to the pseudo-scientific nonsense she'd written? She looked at how many pages were left. Not a lot. She wrote:

Are you the writer?

She turned the page.

I was.

She hadn't expected that particular response, but had expected it to be brief.

> *Look, I don't want to sound rude, but I don't exactly have unlimited space to work with here. I understand things are bad and I get the feeling you're not exactly having a picnic, either, but come on, can't you use more of the page? Answer my questions more thoroughly? Tell me what the hell is going on? I mean, look at it from my point of view. Am I real? Do I just think I'm real? Did you create me and then forget about me? You're kind of like God, you know. So, are you there, God? It's me, Felice, and now that I have a direct line how about some answers and skip the cryptic fortune cookie BULLSHIT. Deal?*

She turned the page.

Help me.

"Goddammit!" She threw the pad, which skittered along the parking lot floor. "YOU-dammit!" Then she remembered the startled young boys nearby. "Darn! Gosh! Jeeze! Golly!"

She was tired of being jerked around. *Help me.* As if. Like he or she or it needed help.

It. Now that was a weird thought. What if some four-headed mono-gendered tripedal creature was writing pulp science fiction about dual gendered bipeds with only one head (how farfetched is *that*, its friends would say, shaking their collective neck-sacks in pity).

She shook herself off the tangent. She didn't even know it was *the* writer of the book. It was just as logical (which was to say not at all) for it to be a ghost instead (ghost writer—ha!).

And yet, she knew. What was more, she knew it was a he, possibly because of the sloppy handwriting.

She picked up the Gideon to check what was happening in Agent Groves-land. When she opened it, one of the burnt fragments she'd salvaged from the hermit's safe fell onto her lap. She'd forgotten about them. It would take ages to sort through them all. She looked to Mikey and his new friend and smiled.

"Hey, when you're done with the cards, I've got a puzzle for you." She shook the Gideon a few inches off the ground so all the fragments fell into a small pile.

"These are bits and pieces from several different stories. I want you to see if you can find out which pieces belong to the same stories, maybe even what order they belong in. You'll have to use your imaginations, though. There are huge gaps between each piece."

The card house must have been getting boring because their faces lit up at the project. Ah, kids. Turn something into a game or claim it's fun and you can trick them into doing all kinds of mundane work. Thank you, Tom Sawyer. Good thing there were no video games around.

She went to get her notebook off the floor, but was beaten to it by Agent Groves. He gave her a '*You kneed me in the balls and I'm not sure I like you anymore*' look—a surprisingly exact expression that involved partial use of his signature eyebrow arch.

Felice had to admit she felt awkward. It hadn't really been his fault, after all, and she wasn't exactly innocent.

"Mr. Groves, er, Agent Groves, um, can I call you David?"

"Probably not."

"Fair enough. Look, I'm sorry. I overheard what you were saying to your friends and I'm sorry. I got angry. I was lonely but I didn't want to accept the idea of us being two ships passing in the night. Monogamy, and all that. Call it a religious hang-up."

Groves's face was impassive, then cracked a small grin. "Don't worry about it. I figured you had to have heard me somehow and, well, locker room talk has never been PC. The truth is, though, I was already interested in someone, but I didn't think she'd give me the time of day. After your little reality check, I—"

Felice waved for him to stop. "I know. I know. Doc McKay was still blushing when I saw her."

"So I'm sorry, too. And I should thank you. I hope you don't mind."

Felice hid a smile. "I can honestly say you two were made for each other."

"She seems more like my opposite to me, but thanks." He paused and looked at the notepad. It was a on a blank page. "There's another reason I'm here."

"What is it?"

"We're going to salvage the bus from the parade route, bring it back here, but it seems no matter how quiet we think it is out there, trouble always finds us." Groves's tone worried her, but she agreed to help. Mikey would be safe here and she needed to feel useful. "Do you know where Pine Street is?" Felice shook her head. He drew a quick map of the area on her notebook, showing where the bus was and the route they'd have to take. Felice was going to protest his using her notepad, but he'd already started, and complaining about it would only make her look weird. Weird-*er*.

"It's the only clear route between here and the bus, about ten blocks away, halfway back to the Lutz Institute. It should be a cakewalk if it's still running, but chances are it won't. We're bringing everything we need for on-the-spot repair. You seem to know how Moaners behave, so I'd like you with Toby on lookout."

"You don't think I can help repair the bus?"

Groves looked surprised. "I'm sorry. Can you?"

Felice remembered the cruiser by the motel. "Er...no. So, when do we leave?"

"Now. We want it back here before dark." Groves handed her the pad and left. Almost instantly he was stopped by a young man who had a problem that needed his attention. Felice glanced under the map page.

DANGER

"STOP WASTING PAPER!"

Groves looked back and held up his hand, cutting off the man's question mid sentence. "I can get you another pad, Preacher."

"I didn't mean...oh, never mind."

✎✎

There were four other men on the fire team. Felice was the only woman. Toby was there, as well as someone else she recognized from earlier that day. The others were new; one was barely old enough to shave.

Groves addressed the group. He reminded the new guys what he expected of them and went over the route they'd be taking.

"Nick and Sudhir will give the bus a once over and find out what needs to be repaired. As long as we can get it moving, we'll deal with the little stuff back at Haven. Raj, you're with me. Toby, you'll be on the roof providing lookout with the Preacher." Groves pointed at her waist. "Uh, Preacher...is that really necessary?"

Felice looked down at the Gideon. She'd sewn in a belt on both sides so she could wear it like a purse over her shoulder.

"You're not going to need a bible in a firefight, are you?"

The warning from the notepad, vague as it was, was on the forefront of Felice's mind. "More than you might think."

Groves shrugged. He wasn't going to argue. "Let's roll!"

Felice walked for the exit, only to realize everyone else had gone the other way. She turned and saw them pile into a black Escalade SUV.

"Where are you going?" asked Groves.

"Sorry. Just got used to walking everywhere." Groves raised his signature eyebrow. "Sometimes I bicycle," she added.

Groves shook his head. "Come on. Get in."

She climbed into the back. "You guys get smooth jazz FM on that radio?"

"Just W-T-H-H," said the driver. He turned it on as they went up the ramp.

"—to report that Haven's population is up to four-hundred and twenty now, and we've still got room to spare. So, remember, if you see our flag on the street, make contact. We can protect you." While DJ spoke, Toby unfurled their red flag on the passenger side and hung it out the window. "Now, I'm afraid something wiped our iPod, so I don't have any music for you, so until the next update I'll be reading from Carl Sagan's Cosmic Connection—"

After a few minutes, Groves told the driver to cut the radio. "We're almost there."

Up ahead was the parade route, just as deserted as before. Felice referred to the Gideon—nothing new.

They parked and formed outside the bus. Felice and Toby scampered to the roof of the bus with their weapons and binoculars. Each took a different end of the bus. As before, Toby had the flag strapped under his rifle; it leaned on his shoulder as he scanned his half of the street. The others got to work.

"Slashed tire over here," Raj called out.

From inside the bus, Nick said, "Gas is okay. Battery's good."

Felice heard Groves ask, "Will it start?"

"Only one way to find out." The engine whirred but didn't catch. Sudhir was looking under the hood. "Checking the fuel line."

"Don't bother. It's the starter," said Groves.

Felice continued to glance at the Gideon, looking for a clue the reader was supposed to know before the characters. The fact everything she'd just heard was repeated on the page meant something was about to go down.

"Get ready, Toby. I've got a bad feeling about this."

Nothing happened. Then she thought she saw movement a few blocks away. "Did you see that?"

Toby followed Felice's gaze, but shook his head. "You sure?"

Felice saw the movement again, just past a ruined float. She checked through the binoculars. Multiple figures were moving in their direction. "Something's coming!"

This time Toby nodded. "Got it." He leveled his rifle and checked through the scope. "They look okay." He stomped on the roof three times. "Survivors incoming!"

Felice saw about twenty people making their way to the bus, led by a thin woman with long brown hair. She had a hunted look about her, but stood out for what she carried instead of a weapon. A book.

When they got closer, she waved her people onward and stopped to check its pages. Felice's jaw dropped. She raised her binoculars to make sure she wasn't seeing things. She wasn't. Felice checked her Gideon, assuming the woman knew something she didn't. It only briefly mentioned the group approaching the bus.

When she looked up from the pages, the other woman stared at her in equal disbelief. The woman held her book overhead, and in a moment of profound camaraderie, Felice did the same. They waved as if they'd each found an old friend. Not a word could be heard at this distance, not with the noise the survivors made, but she knew she'd found another like herself. A void was being filled; it felt like they stood a chance. A real chance.

Then a black and orange streak flew into the woman and smashed her into the wall. Dust and brick flew everywhere, leaving a gaping hole behind. Felice couldn't believe what she'd seen.

No. Not now!

She jumped from the bus to the hood of a smashed car, then ran for the building, pushing past the screaming survivors running the other way. There was a shriek, a howl and a bright flash from the hole, then nothing. When Felice reached it, Mel stepped out.

Without thinking, Felice aimed her shotgun, but Mel batted it out of her hand with such force it drove the weapon through a car windshield.

Mel grabbed Felice by the throat. She looked younger than before, and skankier. Definitely skankier. As if there hadn't been enough surprises today, Mel jumped up into the air with her, and didn't bother coming back down.

The bitch could *fly* now?

Felice was slowly being strangled by her own weight, dangling dozens of feet in the air. Mel behaved like she did this sort of thing all the time, but didn't feel the need to show it off.

"You, I remember. You found my mole. Who are you?"

But Felice was used to reality stepping sideways on her and didn't take long to get her mental footing back. She reached for her sidearm.

Mel said, "I think I'll keep you in a fridge somewhere, for later."

The Glock fumbled in Felice's hand, until she managed to get a grip. She knew it was pointless. Mel had taken a hundred bullets at the bowling alley and just gotten up, but maybe it would distract her. She brought the gun to the hell-woman's head.

Mel did something unexpected. She gasped. Instead of taking the bullet, she grabbed the barrel with her free hand. They struggled in the air, suspended by nothing more than Newton's laws going on vacation.

Then Mel's eyes went hollow and she thrust her face toward Felice.

Felice saw nothing, but heard the violent rushing of wind and fury all around her. She felt cold and kept getting colder. All hope, all joy, all mirth drained away, replaced by a void of nothingness and the fear that what lay beyond was much worse.

With one last bit of conscious thought, Felice made a focused single effort to kick Mel's uterus up into her teeth. Mel's head snapped back, and Felice was out of the void. She would treasure the pained expression and confusion on Mel's face—for about two seconds.

Then Mel lost her grip, and Newton's laws wandered back from vacation with a nice tan and a bad hat.

Felice fell.

People often talk about time slowing down in moments of crisis, but this was different. Time had been different in the void, and for a moment that carried over with Felice. She had as much time as she needed to realize it had been a *really* bad idea to try and make the person holding her high up in the air let go. She realized even if she somehow didn't go splat on the pavement she would suffer the same fate as Gordon the stockbroker. And she knew she didn't want that bitch doubled over in mid-air to get away with it.

Felice aimed her Glock and fired as she fell. The bullets moved so slow she could see them. It didn't seem to help with her aim any, but Mel's head did flinch once. The further she fell the more time sped up, until at last she caught up with reality—just in time for her to create a two foot dent in the roof of the school bus.

The festival in Görlitzhafen was the biggest and brightest Lia could remember. And for the first time since the Great Drought, she was allowed to perform for an audience. She wondered if her sister might be among them.

She had practiced her small part all alone for so long. In the forests, she never thought she'd have a chance to perform again. Now that her time had come, her heart raced and threatened to burst from her chest. She started for the stage when she heard the clatter of metal and an innocent, "Uh oh."

A small girl had found her way backstage, and had been rummaging through a prop chest. She wore a conical Pileus cap so big it covered her eyes, along with a small buckler divided into red, white, black and yellow quadrants. The sword she had been trying to hold lay on the floor in front of her.

"Oh ho," said Lia, arms crossed. "I found a thief! I shall have to call the guards at once."

The girl peeked at Lia from under the cap, shrieked, dropped the props back in the trunk and ran away. Lia smiled and returned to the stage. Time to put on a show.

Most of those attending clustered around the open stage, milling about as final preparations were made. Lia looked at the mask in her hand. She wondered if she should walk out wearing it, or try something different—perhaps come out on stage without it on, then don the mask with a dramatic flourish.

The screams she heard were too far away to be connected to the show, but even before the curtain rose, she could tell something was wrong. A drunken brawl that had turned to bloodshed, perhaps. What a wonderful way to mark her return.

The musicians in front of the stage announced the start of the play. Lia decided to be daring, and walked out as she was, mask in hand. Before she could raise it, however, she saw the crowd was no longer paying attention to her. They'd turned to disturbance by the stables, which had grown louder. The lights had gone out, and shambling figures came toward them.

They moaned, and their faces were like masks.

Felice's eyes flickered open. She felt as though she'd been stomped on with a steel-toed boot the size of a Buick. Everything was gray, but there was something else—long blurry and dark, bisecting her view. She squinted, and a metal pipe swam into focus, running over her head along the ceiling.

"I think she's awake." The voice was muffled, like she was underwater.

"How long does she have? An hour? A day? Talk to me."

"It's impossible to say. I need to run more tests."

Everything was clearer now. She was in Haven, lying on a table. The voices were Doc McKay and Agent Groves. She raised her head and saw two armed men at the foot of the table. Felice was strapped down.

"What the..."

Agent Groves stepped forward, but stayed a good five feet away. "Don't try and move, Preacher. We thought we'd lost you there for a while."

"By all rights, you should be dead," said the Doc. She was off to the side, checking her ray gun. "The bus broke your fall, but you should have broken every bone in your body. Not to mention internal injuries. You're unbelievably lucky."

She didn't feel so lucky. "Why am I strapped down?"

Groves asked, "Do you remember what happened? Before you hit the bus?"

Felice nodded. "That bitch Mel had me. She grabbed me by the throat, flew up in the air...did that really happen?" Groves nodded. "And I kicked her, she let go and...well, *thud*, I guess."

"Do you remember what happened before you kicked her?"

Dark. Cold. Hope, joy, mirth, all lost to the void.

"She got me, didn't she?" Again, Groves nodded. "How long before I'm one of *them?*"

"We're not sure," said Groves. "We got you here as fast as we could. I thought maybe Doc's machine—"

McKay cut him off. "He thought it might be used to destroy the QROC field before it consumed you."

Felice groaned. They'd used that Star Trek prop reject on her, hadn't they?

McKay continued, "And he was right, it might. I subjected you to as broad a range of frequencies as I could, since we didn't know the exact—"

Felice tuned out the techno-babble that followed. Really, who needed it? When it was over she asked, "So am I cured?"

The Doc and FBI agent exchanged uneasy glances. "Probably not," said Groves.

Doc McKay said, "At the most we may have stabilized you. The way Terry was. But eventually..."

Felice remembered the chapter where Terry lost control and killed a survivor. He hadn't meant to; the void took over and all he could do afterward was try to hide the truth. Ignore the voice inside his head. Mel's voice. Was she in there now, watching? Using her as a spy? Laughing? "Which is why I'm strapped down."

Agent Groves nodded. "The Doc is trying everything, but the fact is we just can't be sure. Maybe once she knows the exact quantum frequency..."

Felice tried not to roll her eyes. "I get it. Keep hope alive, right?"

Groves forced an encouraging smile that spoke volumes in the opposite direction.

There was no hope. This wasn't that kind of story. She was just the fourth of four state troopers who should have died in the first act, but somehow slipped through the net. She was someone who had learned too much about the way the world worked; little things such as people like her didn't make it out alive. At best, the lessons learned by her death would save Groves and the Doc somewhere toward the end. There was no hope. Not for her.

Groves seemed to sense this. "The Doc wants to try some experiments. Find something that will help us after we escape the city. Will that be okay?"

He was asking her permission? What the heck did they want to do to her? He didn't look like he thought it was a good idea. She wished there was some way she could know what she should do...

There was.

"Look, there might be a way for me to tell if I'm okay or not. Or if these experiments are the right thing to do."

Groves frowned. "How?"

"Bring Mikey down here. Have him bring my bible."

Doc McKay shook her head, but refrained from any overt religious cracks. "I don't think that will—"

"Just do it. It'll only take five minutes."

Groves gave in and had Mikey brought down. Too late, she realized the boy might not react well to her current situation. Panic was set into his face, and he clutched the book like a teddy bear.

"Why is Mom tied up? What's wrong with her?"

He called her Mom. What had she done?

Groves did his best to calm the boy down. "She's sick, Mikey. We're trying to help her get better."

Felice realized they weren't about to unstrap her so she could read the book. Groves took the Gideon from Mikey. "I noticed you kept looking at the book on the bus. I assume you think you've found some sort of code in the pages?" He opened it at the bookmark.

Felice's jaw fell. "Wait, no!" She shut her eyes and held her breath, waiting for the end of everything.

Groves read for a moment. "What's a Tet-Rarch?"

Felice opened one eye. The world hadn't imploded yet. "What did you say?"

"*Tet-Rarch*. Sorry. Am I pronouncing it wrong?"

"What are you reading?"

"'Now in the fifteenth year of the reign of Tiberius Caesar, Pontius Pilate being governor of Judea, Herod being tetrarch of Galilee, his brother Philip tetrarch of Iturea and the region of Trachonitis, and Lysanias tetrarch of Abilene...'"

"Let me see that!" She struggled against the restraints to no avail. Groves held the book close to her face so she could read. She couldn't believe her eyes. It was Luke, apparently, but where she left the bookmark had been just when they were on the school bus. "Go back to the beginning."

Groves flipped back. "You're missing a page," he said.

"I know. Let me see."

CHAPTER 3

Now the serpent was more cunning than any beast of the field which the LORD God had made. And he said to the woman, "Has God indeed said,

'You shall not eat of every tree
of the garden'?"

2. And the woman said to
the serpent, "We may eat the fruit
of the trees of the garden;

3. but of the fruit of the
tree which is in the midst of the
garden, God has said, 'You shall
not eat it, nor shall you touch it,
lest you die.'"

Felice looked at the book, the ceiling, her restraints. Maybe she
was really in a mental hospital recovering from some sort of breakdown. It made a strange kind of sense. Maybe this was an elaborate
fantasy in her broken mind. The city, the people, even Mikey.

He had his school hat on today, even though he still wore the
Better Dead Than Red shirt. A thought occurred to her.

"Groves, look at Mikey's hat. What school did he go to?"

At this point, Groves didn't bother to argue. He leaned in and
looked at the emblem. "St. Bartholomew's."

Felice laid her head back. There had to be some kind of logic
to this somewhere. If there was she couldn't see it. Not now, not like
this. There was no hope for her, anyway. But maybe she could still
give hope to someone else.

She asked to speak to Agent Groves alone. The guards backed
off and Doc McKay took Mikey back to their room.

"Mikey," she said, looking at Agent Groves. "Promise me you'll
take care of my son."

"He's safe here, and he'll be with us when we get the caravan
out of Fort Rock. I'll have Toby keep an eye on him."

Felice pleaded with him. "*No.* Promise me *you* will take care of
him. Not Toby, not McKay, not someone else. YOU."

Agent Groves seemed to struggle between what he wanted to
say and what he had to do. "I can't."

Anger swelled inside her. "Listen. You're going to run all kinds
of tests on me, and I'll bet money they are going to hurt like hell.
And in the end, I'm going to end up like one of *them* anyways, so I
think I'm entitled to one last bit of hope."

Groves looked away. For the first time Felice saw despair on his face, like he knew something she didn't. He shook his head and recited something she'd read before. "*It would come to blows between the giants,*" he said, then looked back at her. "None of us have much hope, Preacher, even if we make it out of Fort Rock. But we have to try. I have five hundred people to take care of. I have to find a way for everyone to get out of here alive, including your son."

"He doesn't need his diapers changed, Groves. He needs someone he can go to when he's scared, or has a question, or just wants a goddamned hug. Someone who would take a bullet to make sure those *things* don't touch him. Are you telling me you're not that man?"

The only thing Felice could hear was the sound of her own rapid breathing.

At last, Groves nodded. "I promise to keep your son safe."

Felice gave a relieved sigh and relaxed. "Then the Doc can do whatever the hell she wants to me."

The experiments weren't painful at first. Often they were laughable, consisting of the Doc pointing what looked like Christmas decorations and nightclub party lasers at her. Whenever she was asked if she felt any different, Felice had to resist the urge to sing "Staying Alive." She didn't want to piss off the only person trying to help her, but it was hard to take stuff that resembled New Age crystal light therapy seriously.

Then the Doc hooked up electrodes to her head.

That was less fun.

After several hours, she was allowed to rest. It was past midnight topside and the Doc had other things to do. Aside from a single guard she was left alone, strapped down to the table.

Eventually, feeling alone in the world, she fell asleep.

Felice panted by the bank of a babbling brook in the midst of a dense forest. Her lungs burned but she couldn't rest yet. *They* couldn't be far behind. They were everywhere. Perhaps they would lose her scent when she crossed the water.

She splashed through, kicking drops high into the air. The world seemed so much bigger around her. She padded her way up a dark hill covered in dead leaves, exhausted, and collapsed at the top. A lone man tended a small fire nearby, his hooded face turned from her. A strange blue dome stood some yards away.

"It wasn't supposed to be like this."

Felice looked around. This wasn't right. "What's going on? Where am I?" Her voice was too high pitched to be her own. A child's voice.

"A few miles west of Görlitzhafen. The site of her first victory."

This was a dream. Felice didn't seem to have much control over her actions.

"Whose?"

The hooded figure poked at the embers with a stick, causing them to flare. "Taker of hope. Bringer of death. The hell woman. The mad god."

Felice shuddered. If Mel was a god then they were screwed. Gods set the tune the players had to dance to. And if they decided your time was up? Mere mortals never stood a chance. They weren't supposed to.

"We are all trapped in her grasp," said the man. "Even me."

"Who are you?"

The hood rose to look at her, but Felice saw only darkness within.

"Her first victim."

DAY 6

Felice awoke to something tugging her arm. She didn't see anyone. Even the guard was gone. Then a small crown of brown hair poked up over her elbow, just as one of the restraints loosened.

"Mikey?" Even as she said it, she couldn't believe it. "What are you doing?" The strap popped open in case it hadn't been obvious enough. "Stop that!" Her voice was a hoarse whisper.

"We have to go. The bad people are here."

Felice looked around. The entire floor was deserted. "Where are they?"

"Outside. They all went out by the big doors. We have to go." He undid another strap. Now she could hear the faint popping of gunfire. They must be down the street.

Felice sat up and took care of the other straps herself. "Mikey, listen. You have to go. You can't be near me. Go find Agent Groves and stay close to him. He can keep you safe."

"I want to stay with you."

"I can't protect you anymore. I might hurt you, even if I don't want to."

She couldn't look directly at him, at the pain in those hazel eyes. He raised a red backpack. "I brought your bag. I don't want to stay here anymore. We have to go back to the motel."

"This is safer than the motel. Agent Groves has a plan to get everyone out of the city, and you're going with him."

"But you're coming too, right?"

"I'm sorry. I might hurt you. I might hurt everyone."

That didn't seem to matter. "But, but, where will you go?" Mikey began to hyperventilate. "I—I want to—come with you!"

"No."

"But Mom, the man said—"

"NO!" Felice clenched her jaw. "I'm not your mom, Mikey." She felt sick saying those words. Her hands shook. "Don't call me that. I'm *not* your mom, but these people, *all* of them, they are your family now."

Mikey's lip quivered, his eyes blurred with tears. Felice slid off the table. She grabbed the backpack with one hand and Mikey's wrist with the other and ignored his cries as she dragged him up to the second floor. There were civilians here; those who, for whatever reason, couldn't fight. She handed the boy off to a middle-aged woman named Susan who'd given them biscuits (Mikey had her write in the notepad that her husband was on a business trip in Hollywood).

"Keep him here until Agent Groves picks him up. Don't let him leave." She heaved the backpack onto her shoulders.

"Mom!" Mikey cried out. "Don't go, Mom! Don't leave me! *MOM!*"

Felice ran her sleeve over her eyes, ignoring the dampness on her face, and didn't look back.

On the first floor were a couple dozen people. Most manned barricades by the garage doors. The fighting could be heard clearly now. The ground shook with a sudden explosion.

One of the men by the recently un-dented school bus—which now read *St. Bartholomew's School*—recognized her. "Preacher? You're not supposed to—" He didn't seem to know if he was supposed to shoot her or not. "Agent Groves said—"

"Where is he?" The man pointed toward a supply room. Groves and two others were headed for the ramp to the surface with a shopping cart full of ammo. When he saw her, he stopped and drew his weapon, but didn't point it at her.

"How did you get out?"

"Mikey. He didn't know any better."

"You know I can't let you run around free, Preacher. Especially not now."

"I don't intend to. Just give me a gun and let me take the front line. I'll be easy to shoot if I turn. Hell, give me a grenade or two and let me charge into them. Just remember your promise."

"Not going to happen. I have no way of knowing if *she's* in your head or not, like Terry."

Felice's eyes narrowed. "Fine. But I'm guessing you won't say no to a live decoy. I'll see if I can draw some of them away from you."

Groves looked her over, then gestured to the others to take the cart and go on without him. "You realize you have no shoes on."

Felice looked down. She was only wearing socks. "Wait a sec." She took off the daypack. Gideon, notepad, food...she fished out the moccasins from the hermit's lair and put them on. "I'll probably run faster in these anyway."

"What about your bible?"

Felice had left out the reset Gideon when she repacked the bag. "Won't need it where I'm going."

Groves gave in. "Okay, fine. You want to throw your life away, who am I to argue?"

"I've got one more favor to ask. Next time you see me, if I'm all..." She pulled down the corners of her eyes so they drooped. "Make sure Mikey doesn't see me like that. Okay? Make it quick."

Groves nodded. "I have to get back to the fight."

"Lead the way."

The surface was a war zone. A block away two hundred men and women faced off against two thousand Moaners, and those were only the ones that were left. The battle had raged so long they used Moaner corpses like sandbags to block the road from end to end.

"They showed up about an hour ago," said Groves. "Few of them are running, though. It's like they're getting weaker. Damned if I know why, but it's the only reason we're still alive." He shouted to Toby, who lay on the roof of a car with his sniper rifle. "How's it going?"

Toby's eye never left the scope. "This looks like the last wave, but it's the biggest yet!" He popped off a shot that took down three Moaners in a straight line.

"Doc's machine holding up?"

"It's almost fried. Says she's got one more shot before it needs a complete overhaul."

"You've got to be kidding me," said Felice. "That pile of junk *works?*"

"Does it ever!" Toby lined up another shot and fired.

"I don't believe it."

"Believe it," said Groves. "It doesn't look like much, but she took down fifty with the first shot alone." For a moment, the determination he wore like a badge faded. "Doesn't matter if we win today, though, they know where we are. All of them. There could be ten times as many Moaners still out there. Once we get the Doc's weapon mounted on the bus, we'll have to make our move. We'll take as many as we can, but..." He didn't finish the sentence, but Felice knew they were at least one bus short. Instead, he pointed to Doc McKay, who had the ray gun set up on another smashed car.

"I'll tell her to clear you a path," said Groves. "You do...whatever you feel you gotta do." The awkward moment was made more awkward when he added, "I'd give you a hug, but...you know, the whole face sucking thing."

"Yeah. Guess that's the Doc's job now, huh?"

Groves smiled. "Be careful."

Felice ran to the front line over the din of gunfire.

"Preacher!" Groves shouted. She turned back and he threw her his sidearm, a Glock 22 like her old one. He gave her a nod. "Kick some ass for the Lord!"

Felice smiled and nodded back.

The men and women at the front line were too busy shooting and reloading to care about Felice. Moaners filled the street from one sidewalk to the other. For every one they dropped another waited, but barring reinforcements the end was in sight.

An air horn blasted three times. Everyone took cover, as did Felice, and a wide bright blue beam shot over her head, swept left and right and went out.

Felice got up and saw a ten-foot wide path covered in ash and Moaner corpses.

"I *still* don't believe it works." She leaped over the barricade of bodies and sprinted through the opening before it filled.

"They're probably just stunned by how stupid it is."

A Moaner lunged at her from an alley. Felice dropped it with two shots to the chest.

"Maybe Moaners can die laughing."

Two more broke away from the main pack and shambled toward her. She emptied four more rounds into them.

"It's just a goddamned TOY!" she yelled at the top of her lungs.

That attracted the attention of several dozen from all sides. More than she had bullets for.

"Whoops."

The Moaners gave chase, managing a short burst of speed just for her. Felice shot two that got close, but the others eventually slowed and were drawn back to the losing battle. By the time she ran out of breath, she couldn't even hear shots anymore.

She looked around. She'd ended up at the abandoned parade route. She could see where the school bus had been, and beyond that, the hole Mel had made in a building, crashing into that other survivor at inhuman speed.

She didn't want to see what was left of the woman, yet something drew her toward the rubble. On some level, she knew it had to be important.

Felice kept forgetting most of the city had no power; it was dark inside, but enough light spilled in to see the broken ruins. She should have expected to see a shattered and rotting corpse on the ground with dried blood everywhere, or at least a hollow Moaner husk. But part of her knew what she'd actually find: a pile of loose clothes. On top she saw what she thought was another Gideon. Only it wasn't. It was the Complete Works of Chaucer. Felice frowned. This, the hermit, and Yuri's story shared the same elements—this was a pattern.

Felice looked at the book next to the clothes, then cautiously reached to pick it up. Her Gideon had reverted to an ordinary bible. It was no accident it had done so when Groves read from it, just as Mikey's nameless private school had become St. Bartholomew's.

It was quantum or something, an unobserved waveform collapsing. Groves was the protagonist, the world around him could be vague and generic but once he paid attention to it—bam.

Bam. Her hand flinched from the book as she considered this. Just how safe *were* you really around Agent Groves?

She looked at the book on Chaucer again and opened it. It was worth a shot.

> "O speak, sweet bird, I know not where thou art."
> This Nicholas just then let fly a fart
> As loud as it had been a thunder-clap,
> And well-nigh blinded Absalom, poor chap;

If that was in any way connected to her situation, she didn't see how. Felice turned back to the beginning. The first few pages were missing.

There was no reason to stay, but she couldn't leave without

some kind of acknowledgment to the pile of clothes. She laid the book down on top of them, the closest thing to a tombstone this woman would ever get.

"I'm sorry we never met," said Felice. "I think we'd have had a lot to talk about."

There was only one place to go now, and on foot, it would take the better part of a day to do so. She'd be lucky to get there before nightfall. With a heavy sigh, she left the rubble.

About fifty yards farther down the road, she found the pink bicycle Mikey had ditched. A sound escaped her lips that might have been a laugh or a sob.

～～

She left the bicycle propped outside motel room 104. Everything was just the way she'd left it. There were enough supplies for a couple of weeks, but she doubted she'd last that long. She'd picked up a new Gideon from another room, oddly relieved to find the fall of Fort Rock back where it belonged. One way or another, things were coming to an end. Even if she didn't become a Moaner, the Gideon re-write was closing in on Revelation.

What would happen then? She understood enough about stories to know loose ends were usually tied up.

She was a loose end.

She pulled the Glock from her holster and considered tying it up herself. All it would take was one bullet. By the time she felt the change, it would be too late, all she was doing by selfishly clinging to life was put everyone else in danger.

If she had to guess the future, she'd bet on becoming one of *them* by morning and shamble back to Fort Rock in search of Mikey. Agent Groves would show up conveniently in time to put a bullet in her heart before she could grab him. Or maybe she would manage to get hold of Mikey first and have his screaming face inches away from hers, then get stabbed in the back by Groves. Something stupid and dramatic like that.

So why not remove that possibility? The answer was maddeningly simple, and meaningless. Hope. Despite everything some hope remained. Maybe the stupid machine *had* worked on her. She'd seen it cut down dozens of Moaners, after all. And even if she did turn, she doubted she'd actually kill anyone. Groves would take her down before she could. Then he, the Doc and Mikey would drive off into the sunset. The End.

There was a whole other question: what happens after The End? Felice thought about the spare tire she'd rolled beyond the city limits, and wondered if that was everyone's fate.

Did the story reset? Would she go through this again and again for eternity? Maybe she had a thousand times before, and each time she was as oblivious as the last.

Something told her this wasn't the case. There had been those dreams. That other place. That other time. What was that all about?

Felice got off the bed and began pacing. She looked at Groves's pistol again, then set it on the nightstand. She was torn between wandering beyond the city limits into oblivion, blowing her brains out, sleeping until the change took place, waiting for the world to end, and trying to solve this damn riddle. The situation was beyond frustrating, but only one of her choices was in any way productive.

She rummaged through the backpack and found the notes from the hermit's bunker. Mikey and his friend had taped them onto blank sheets of paper and set them into a duo-tang like a school project.

As she read the fragments, her eyes widened. A pattern began to emerge, and something she'd suspected in the pit of her stomach was drawn into the light of day.

> "...can't keep the truth hidden forever. The people have a right to know!"
>
> Inspector Mullan groaned. This reporter was really getting on his nerves. What could he tell her? That the world had gone mad and if she wasn't careful she'd be next? He waved her off and...
>
> "...we've got Fifth and Rockafeller blocked off, sir," the policeman said over the car radio. "But we can't be sure they won't find another way around. Hell, they could be on the..."
>
> ...when the Moaners broke through the barricade, Inspector Mullan swore under his breath. All the riot gear in the world wouldn't stop them. It was time to fall back...
>
> ...supposed to do that when there's no way off Manhattan? Tell me that!" The captain scowled

and threw down the report. Mullan didn't answer. "The whole island is in lockdown! Every bridge is blown and the military won't let a boat get within a thousand yards of the shore. So just what are we...

...Private Fairview screamed as the Moaners poured into the trench. It had been a wave even a cross fire of machine-guns hadn't been able to cut down. Their faces looked far worse than anything the posters back home portrayed. Fairview ran back, looking for the cross-trench that would get him to the second line. Maybe they...

...no circumstances was Vimy to remain in the hands of the Huns. Blast and damnation, didn't H.Q. Realize what the real terror was they faced here? At least the Huns were...

...without support for at least two weeks. What were they supposed to do? Six of his friends had come down with the forgetting disease; one had already died—then had to die a second time. To say nothing of the refugees trying to find a way out. How could this get worse?

...a jolly good day for a family outing. Anglesea was an idyllic resort, with an old castle converted into a hotel, tennis courts and lawn bowling, and plenty of beaches all around. Otto smiled at his wife and gave her a wink as the train carried them toward the small island. He'd promised to...

...a revolution I say!" said Lady P. Otto deigned to contain his vitriol as the diva babbled on. "The lower classes have risen up under Lenin's flag, I just know it!"

Otto tried to be diplomatic. "I don't believe communists pluck out their own eyes, my Lady. Yet there is danger, and we must...

...on the locomotive screamed as it crashed off the bridge, taking with it the only way off this god forsaken island. "Heaven preserve us," said

Otto. "That was…"

…Otto hung his head sadly. Of the Lady P. he found nothing save her dress and the book of hymns she always kept close laying on her veil. Since her breakdown, she'd been nearly prophetic, anticipating the movements of…

"…oh the Cardinal is a vile man, but he has his uses," said the queen. "If he says there is danger, I have no doubt that there is. The question is, for whom?"

Terpé saw the cloud that had passed over her queen's face. "Shall I sing for you?"

The queen smiled to her lady-in-waiting. "Not all problems can be solved in song, Terpé."

"Is it insurrection you fear, your majesty?"

"Perhaps. We will play his game a little longer. Send a messenger to…"

…queen strode through the courtyard. She ordered her musketeers to hold the line, no matter the cost, lest these horrors breach the inner sanctum and…

…with the Cardinal's smug look of a man playing a game straight to the ends of the earth and the depths of hell. It took all her will not to snap Terpé's flute in half. Her love for her lost confidant stayed her hand—but not her temper. "Enough! These…unholy abominations, these… moaning damned that fill the street with blood and ash, have infiltrated my own castle, the witch that leads them killed my lady in waiting—and you say you have nothing to do with…

…she came to the festival full of wonder and desire. The city of Görlitzhafen was so alive, so full of life and opportunity; she knew she had to have it. She wanted everything the city had to offer. Everything…

…musicians beneath the stage announced

the start of the play. She decided to be daring, and walked onto the stage as she was, mask in hand. Before she could raise it to her face, however, she saw that the crowd was not paying attention to her. They all watched the disturbance by the stables, where the lights had gone out, as shambling figures came toward them.

They moaned, and their faces were like masks...

There was more, but she had read enough.

It was a cycle, but not the kind she'd expected.

Had the hermit known? She must have. She had written the stories down herself and locked them away in her safe, or tried. And someone—perhaps Miss Cleo herself when she knew who was coming for her—had tried to destroy them.

Felice's eyes narrowed. The bitch wasn't just the antagonist. Somehow, she was *part* of this. Right from the start in Görlitzhafen—she'd seen it through Mel's own eyes at one point, like she'd been watching from a video camera. And she'd seen it through someone else's eyes. An actress, maybe? A child? She wrapped her head trying to remember. There had been a stage involved, just before it all went wrong in a very familiar way. So much she didn't know. So much just out of her grasp. She needed answers.

Her thoughts drifted back to the notebook. Of course! She had enough to work with now that even the cryptic S-O-B on the other side of the page couldn't evade her questions. She pulled the pad from her backpack and started flipping through pages of character sketches and questions with brief unhelpful answers until she found where she left off.

There was a pencil drawing of a house. It was a sunny day; stretched out m's that were supposed to be seagulls hung on the page next to a single puffy cloud. By the house were two crude stick figures. The little one had a cap on and said "Mikey" underneath.

The bigger one had a rectangle for a book in one hand and an L-shaped box for a gun in the other. Underneath it said "Mom." She had a big smile on her face, like it was perfectly normal to carry a bible and gun around.

She turned the page. Her vision began to blur. She regretted ever telling Mikey she wasn't his mother. She'd written it down. As far as she was concerned, that made it a fact. She wiped her eyes with her sleeve.

The next page had only three words in the center in a familiar messy handwriting:

I'm so sorry.

Felice wondered for a moment if whoever was on the other side of the page had somehow read her mind. She turned the page to write a question but instead saw an even messier hand had beaten her to it.

Can you help my mom?

Felice gasped. Mikey had figured out the notebook. It probably took a child's mind to not only accept it as plausible, but pick up on it without missing a beat. She turned the page. As before, each question needed a fresh page to answer.

You have to get her out.

Why?

It's not safe. You have to leave.

Where do we go?

Bring her to me.

Where are you?

Room 104.

The notebook slipped from Felice's fingers. She didn't want to lift her head or move her gaze because she knew this would be the perfect time for some hooded figure with no face to have been standing in the room all along, watching her.

But there was no such person. She was alone. Heart still racing she picked up the notebook and found a pen. One blank page left, so under *Room 104* she wrote:

I'm here. Now what?

She turned the page.

Sleep.

Felice frowned. Easier said than done. With no warm milk, turkey, or countable sheep handy, Felice tried to tire herself with exercise, jogging around the motel while the sun set. At least it helped clear her head. Eventually she was able to collapse on the bed in exhaustion, but even then it was long dark before she began to drift.

She looked out the large windows, having forgotten to close the blinds, and for the first time she could remember, saw the full night sky. So many stars, and the cloudy band of their own galaxy. Even in her exhausted state, it was impossible not to be moved. She remembered what Yuri had said.

You can see them all. You can see the Milky Way. Sit still long enough and you can almost feel our little ball of rock rolling slowly through the cosmos. Our world's going to hell, sure, but there are billions and billions of others out there that must be doing okay for themselves. There's some comfort in that.

There was. Felice slept.

A man wrapped in a sheet sat hunched over at the edge of his bed, tapping on a small laptop. The sheet concealed most his face except for a messy beard, maybe a couple months old.

His fingers shook as he typed in spurts. Several sentences would flow, followed a brief stop—long enough to collect his thoughts—before he started again. His arms looked thin, and the bumps of his spine made small shadows down his back along the length of the sheet. His breathing became labored at times. Once in a while, he coughed. He looked like a man who had started chemotherapy a little too late, fighting and dying to the point where they looked more or less like the same thing. The floor was littered with garbage. Junk food wrappers and empty cans of soda were strewn everywhere, as were sheets of paper filled with mad scribbled notes, which looked as if they'd been written by two different hands.

The man had been here for a few weeks, but the motel manager barely remembered what he looked like. The man never came out during the day, and only to the diner at night. For over a week, though, he hadn't done that, either. But as long as the credit card kept clearing and the room didn't start to smell of death, the manager was happy enough to leave him alone like he asked.

The manager had recognized him when he first showed up. Aside from the beard, he didn't look like your average tourist. Most of them were dressed for the outdoors, ready for a big hike or climb. This guy seemed to have picked his clothes at random. The manager had seen him on some talk show his wife watched before her stories. A writer or something. He looked happy and presentable on the tube, but the man that rented room 104 had had a haunted, vacant look. With TV his only link to life in the big city, the manager figured it was drugs. Had to be. Shooting up and writing his way to another bestseller. Typical Californian.

In Room 104, the writer stopped typing. He looked up slowly and stared at the mirror, but not at his reflection. His eyes moved back and forth, sometimes up and down. His body sagged and slumped to the side, eyes still open.

Felice was there. She knelt and looked at his rapidly moving eyes. She wanted to shut them, but knew she couldn't. She was afraid if she stretched her hand out she wouldn't be able to see it, and she really didn't want to deal with something like *that* right now.

"Who are you?" she asked.

Doesn't really matter, does it?

The writer's lips had twitched, but the words hadn't come from them. They seemed to echo inside her own head, assuming her head was even there.

"What's going on? And please, no wise-ass-on-the-mountain using six words or less answers."

She could have sworn she heard a chuckle.

Try rummaging through your own subconscious and see how coherent you are. When the lips stopped twitching, a faint smile cracked on them.

"How is this different for you?"

I think I'm partially conscious. Let's find out. The writer stuck out his tongue ever so slightly. *I might even be able to get up and move, but I'd probably flail about like a zombie.*

"Or a Moaner."

The body let out a deflating sigh. Felice didn't know if it was intentional or a reflex.

I'm sorry. For everything.

"I'd prefer it if you were helpful instead of sorry. Help me. How do I stop that bitch? How do I save Mikey? How do we get out of this?"

Look at me.

Felice had no choice in the matter. She looked at his haggard face, and with the bed sheet partially open, she saw his frailty. She saw his rib cage and a dent where his belly should be. He was sweating, even though he was naked aside from the sheet.

Do I look like I know how to stop this?

"Then why am I here?"

I'm hoping you can save me, and in doing so, save yourself.

"How?"

By stopping the mad god.

"How?"

I don't know.

Felice swore and looked away, trying not to notice she had no reflection in the dresser's mirror. She saw the television, the nightstand, the door to the bathroom. This was the same motel room she was sleeping in, only messier and with electricity.

"What can I do?" said Felice. "I'm in your head. I'm part of you, aren't I? If you can't think of what to do, how can I?"

It's complicated.

"Understatement of the year."

Maybe within my story you'll find a way to survive in yours.

"Do I have a choice in the matter?"

Not really.

"Figures."

Felice knew what she'd seen in her—what could you call it?—out-of-someone-else's-body-experience was real. She was equally certain what she saw next was not. It had the clouded veneer of memory about it. Specific details the writer had paid attention to were in sharp focus, while everything else was vague and subjective. Maybe this was how Agent Groves saw the world, as opposed to those around him, like her. At least Felice could see herself now.

They were in an apartment. The writer was clean-shaven and fifty pounds heavier. He could stand to lose a few, in fact. He was tapping on his computer at a desk in a bedroom. A woman with short black hair who looked like Felice (*no-she-did-not!*) came in and gave him a peck on the cheek. The writer smiled but kept typing.

"What the hell is this?" asked Felice. Neither of the ghosts heard her, of course. "Is that me?"

No, it's not.

The Felice doppelganger handed the writer some mail. He opened them, groaned and said, "Put them with the others."

The doppelganger pulled a box from the closet and put the opened envelopes inside. It was almost full. Before she closed it, Felice managed to read the letter on the top. THANK YOU FOR YOUR SUBMISSION. WE'RE SORRY TO INFORM YOU THAT—

Felice wanted to make some kind of smart-alec remark. Something like, "If the key is boring Mel to death, then you've got your secret weapon right here." But that was a rather rude thing to say to the man who was, for lack of a better term, God. Besides, she had a feeling he would get to the point.

The voice echoed in her head. *What do you know about stories?*

She was still in the room with his younger self typing away. The only thing in sharp focus now was the monitor.

"Everything you do, I would think."

You might be surprised.

Felice had no idea how to answer this. "They start with Once Upon a Time and end with They Lived Happily Ever After." The silence that followed was enough to make her attempt a proper answer. "I know lots. What do you want? Do you want me to tell you of the story of The Soldier and Death? Three Billy Goats Gruff? The Hobbit? Something by Hemingway, perhaps? Wilde? Homer? Do you want me to talk about structure? Characterization? Plot? Symbolism? Metaphor? I told you, I know what you know, so this is a pretty one sided conversation." She paced around the room growing more and more frustrated.

I've never read Hemingway.

That stopped Felice in her tracks. "You're joking."

Never got around to it.

Felice looked around like someone expecting to find a hidden camera. "The Old Man and the Sea?"

No.

"For Whom The Bell Tolls?"

Nope.

"Under Kilimanjaro?"

On my To-Do-List.

"Then how do I know them?"

That's a good question. Do you?

"Maybe you read the Cliff's Notes version for school, or the synopsis on Wikipedia?"

No. I don't have a clue what The Old Man and the Sea is about, aside from what the title implies.

"And you call yourself a writer?"

Now hang on a minute—

Felice couldn't resist. She went over to the ghost-of-author-past and said, "Look at you, tapping away as if you know what the hell you're doing. Aren't you cute?"

The voice was compelled to defend itself. *I never said I don't read. I said I never read Hemingway. I've read hundreds of books. Probably thousands. But he seemed to be on the depressing side, like Steinbeck—who I have read, thank you very much—and I prefer more cheerful stories.*

Felice wondered what she'd have seen if she'd been looking in a mirror. Would her jaw hit the floor, or just reach her bellybutton? "You *do* realize what kind of story you're writing, don't you? It's not about puppies and kittens having playful adventures in Candyland."

The sigh that followed told Felice she was trying his patience. *For years, the only things I read were light comedies and rom-coms because that's what I wanted to write. I wanted to write stuff that someday would be made into a movie starring Meg Ryan or Sandra Bullock.*

"Crap. Gotcha."

Would you please *stop that?*

"Don't blame me. I'm an ambassador from your subconscious, apparently. I claim diplomatic immunity."

Perhaps the author figured it was better to move on than try to win this argument. The surrounding images faded until only the author and the computer remained.

My wife was supportive, of course. She enjoyed my stories, and I enjoyed writing them for her. For a time, that was enough. But I felt like I was letting her down. She never came out and said it, but I believed she wished I'd put it all behind me and get a "real" job.

Felice felt the quote marks float by in her mind.

Mark Twain once said: "Write without pay until someone offers to pay you. If nobody offers within three years, sawing wood is what you were intended for." Every so often, I'd get a short story published, but it was getting to the point where I was looking in the Help Wanted ads for lumberjacks.

But I had gotten this far. I had the skills. I just needed something to make it click. A magic bullet. I looked to history, the storytellers of old, the oral tradition, the playwrights, the troubadours, the places where stories as we know them began. If I could find the source of their inspiration, maybe I could use it, too.

The world was white now except for the author, sitting on a ghost of a chair, working at a mirage of a computer screen.

"Didn't they just work hard at it?"

Of course. But where does that spark come from that tells you this *idea would go really well with* that *one? We see all kinds of stories that just don't work, or are only competent, or are derivative of better stories. When something great comes along, it's not just skill, or luck for that matter. It's another kind of power altogether. One as old as the gods, because* that *is who I summoned.*

"Dun-dun-DUNnnnn!" said Felice.

The ghost-of-author-past stood from his now invisible chair. "Will you knock it off?"

Felice jumped. She hadn't expected that. The author walked toward her and Felice backed away. Fortunately, there was an infinity of emptiness all around, so she could keep it up as long as needed.

"I understand how it sounds," said the author, looking straight at her, straight through her. "But it's not as if I took the matter seriously. I was looking for inspiration, and if it took digging up some old rituals, invoking some dead names, inhaling some questionable burnt herbs, and dressing for a frat house toga party, then so be it. I just wanted to get noticed. And I was. Unfortunately."

Felice continued backing up until they reached the edge of some new set, which took on more and more detail as they moved. First, there was a tree, then a rock, then she heard a splash as she stepped into a stream.

"I said summoned before, but I don't think that's what happened. I think they were waiting for me, or someone like me. The spells, the rituals, it was just so much nonsense. But it demonstrated a willingness, an openness, a *weakness*, a door that could be walked through. Only instead of tidying things up inside, one got mud on the carpet, raided the fridge and forgot to flush the toilet."

She'd now backed up to the top of a hill. The white had receded to become a distant fog. For all intents and purposes, she was in a forest. A strangely familiar forest. When the author spoke again, the voice didn't come from the man in front of her, but behind. She turned and saw the camp from her dream—the one with the hooded man. Only now, she recognized the blue dome as a tent, and the author himself was dressed in a blue padded hiking jacket. He sat on a log by the fire.

"We were living in Europe at the time. I came here, not too far from some caves I'd heard about. I told my wife I needed to get away for a couple of weeks, to write without distractions or a computer. I told her I was going back to basics, but I didn't bother telling her what I planned to do to get there. It was just a new superstition I was trying out. Superstition is simply a way to establish routine, in the hopes that routine leads to focus, which leads to success."

Felice sat on another log across from the writer while he tended the fire.

"So I got stoned, old school, like the Oracle at Delphi. I read the rituals and invoked the names of those I thought could help me, and my voice was heard. That was my undoing."

"The mad god," said Felice.

The author paused, looking deep into the fire, a sadness in his eyes. "No. Not at first. There was another. Someone wonderful. You can't imagine how it felt to have her in my head. I literally held another presence inside me. Curious, friendly, full of wonder, like a child. But also lonely. So lonely for so long. It was like she had been rescued from a desert island and wasn't sure if she could fit back in society."

"Lemuel Gulliver," said Felice, half to herself. "Or Robinson Crusoe."

"Something like that. With her came other feelings and presences, like a parade. I assumed it was all part of the trip, of course; the Colonel's secret blend of eleven herbs and spices. I didn't care. I was awe-struck. I started a new story right away, something set in medieval times, set in the town I'd visited the day before, or something vaguely like it.

"At first I didn't feel anything special happen. I wrote a dozen or so pages the way I normally would, but it didn't seem to be going anywhere. Then I could feel her walk *through* it. It was like I was following her. I didn't see through her eyes, but I saw everything she could with so much clarity. When she spoke to people, they seemed real. I could count the bricks on every building if I wanted to. When I finally took a break it was dark, I hadn't even noticed how much time had passed. I looked at what I had written and it was...good. Not great, but good.

"But what did I expect? I was high, or so I thought, and that's what the edit is for, right? What I had written was mostly setting and character, not a story, but I thought I knew where things were going. I pictured a young woman who wanted to be an actress and the knight who would fall in love with her.

"When I started to write again, I realized the presence had become the actress. It was perfect. I now saw the world vividly around my protagonist. How she prepared, how she was nervous about her first performance. I was barely aware of my pen flying over the pages. I expected the knight would be in the audience watching her, but I never got past the curtain rising and her walking on stage."

Felice spoke up. "That was when the story changed."

"Yes. That was when the Moaners came. When I realized I not only had lost control of the story, but my own body. When I felt the *other's* talons grab hold of my mind. I couldn't control what happened. I simply recorded the events as an impassive witness. And in the end..." The writer jabbed the fire. Hot sparks flew into the air and cooled to ash. "In the end they were all gone. All of them. Two weeks had passed. I was starving. I had eaten everything, but didn't remember doing so. It felt like I hadn't eaten in three days. It was fall, my jacket was off, and yet I was sweating.

"All of my notebooks were full. My hand was cramped and claw like. What I saw in the notebooks looked like it had been written by me, sounded like me, but I didn't remember doing any of it. The last thing I remembered was that first friendly presence at my mind, asking politely to be let in."

The author sighed. "I thought a prayer had been answered, that elves had saved my shoe store. I didn't remember the hell I'd been put through. I saw only the results. Who cared if I was a bit cramped and hungry? I had a book. A fairly entertaining one. So I rushed home and got to editing.

"It turned out I had written twice as much as I needed to. Most of the time I cut maybe ten percent during the second draft, here it was just under fifty. I didn't understand why I had developed so much back story for so many minor characters, but the way I saw it, it was better to have too much and subtract than too little and add."

"She didn't mind?"

"She doesn't care what happens to the words once they've been written. When I was done, I sent it to my agent. She called it a revolution of the horror genre, which meant it was original enough to keep old readers interested, and familiar enough not to scare away new readers.

"It was a hit, and I was screwed. Of course, I didn't realize the latter until much later. My publisher wanted more of the same, but I was vague about my next project. It's not like I expected to write *The Moaners of Görlitzhafen*. Who knew what the next story would look like?

"That spring I set out again for the woods, but I didn't need the ritual. I felt someone inside me, waking up as I laid things out. I didn't realize it was the *other* that slept. I was better prepared this time, with twice the food, twice the paper and countless pens.

"When it was over, I got up to start packing, only to realize my leg hurt like hell. Turned out I broke it in a fall, hairline fracture, and had a gash that got infected. I hadn't done anything to disinfect it. I was lucky I didn't die. But I had another book and lo and behold, it was a sequel to the Moaner story, set a hundred years later.

"After that I was more careful. I rented a hotel the next time. Got a huge room service bill, but it worked out okay. That Moaner book was set during the renaissance. I switched to typing on laptops to speed things up, only to write even more that had to be deleted."

Felice hadn't blinked, she was sure she hadn't. For a split second, the world went black, then the lights were on in a fancy hotel room, the kind with bathrobes you're tempted to smuggle away in your luggage. The author was on the bed. He was thinner, his eyes had dark circles under them, but he looked okay. Nowhere near the wreck she'd found in Room 104.

"The direction the stories went in wasn't intentional at all on my part. I began every book thinking it would be something light and fun this time, but it always turned into another Moaner novel. I always had to ditch the first chapter or two during my edits, because *that* story was completely forgotten."

Felice remembered the missing pages in the Gideon and other books. "What did you start this time?"

"A romantic comedy between an FBI agent and a scientist investigating a string of art frauds." The writer turned on the TV; there he was on a morning talk show. "The Moaner books were successful, but it took its toll on my private life. Every time I do it, it gets worse. Takes a little longer to finish, takes a little more out of me, is just a little harder to get it all back. But I always come out of the trance thinking I still had it under control. My wife saw me come home from these trips two, three times a year, getting thinner, looking more haggard, my eyes just a bit more vacant. She thought I was on drugs, and even though I'd stopped using the herbs, I sort of was. She tried to help, but she chose the worst possible time to intervene—in the middle of a story.

"My wife found the hotel room I was staying at, but it wasn't me who answered the door. *She* told her I had things under control, told my wife to back off before I could snap out of it, which in my sorry state only reinforced the drug theory. In the end, it came down to an ultimatum: my marriage or my books."

He didn't have to say who came out on top. He gave a sigh that carried the regrets of a lifetime.

"This was two books ago. And every time I start writing, this part of me remembers what I'd been put through before. All of it. It's her final twist of the knife, you see, to let me know she got me again. But do you know what is the worst part is? Every time I relive these memories, that last argument with my wife, I expect to see *her* pull the strings, force me to choose the stories. But she's not there.

Of all the things I can blame on her, that isn't one of them. I did that to myself."

The author looked at himself on the television set. "I stopped caring about what *she* was doing to me. Sometimes I look back at myself during those TV interviews, loaded up on cheeseburgers for a month to look human again, and want to give up. That bastard with the smug face, soaking in all the attention, he's getting *exactly* what he deserves.

"But the part of me that remembers I gave up the best thing that ever happened to me because that bitch wants to fight back. The problem is, she dominates the world she helps create. I've tried forcing myself in, changing the rules, changing the characters, changing the plot. It doesn't work. It's like daydreaming at the office, nothing gets done. But I can make subtle changes under her nose. As long as it doesn't become part of the written story, it stays put."

Felice had a flash of insight. "The Gideon."

"I suppose. My focus has been on books. Everyone talks about the 'writer's bible;' the rules our worlds follow. But it's a metaphor. It could have been any book, really. Whatever felt appropriate. I hoped someone would notice, and start piecing things together. I hoped I could make contact somehow. But I think you made contact with me."

"With the notepad."

The writer nodded. "Sometimes her attention is focused elsewhere, doing other things, and her grip isn't so tight. During one of these breaks, if you can call them that, I noticed I'd written something down on the motel notepad with my left hand. They looked like disjointed story notes, from a part of the story I hadn't written. A different perspective. It mentioned a book—a book that told the character what was happening in the story. I didn't know what to do or what it meant, but I could already feel *her* coming back. I scribbled something down and tore out the page."

Felice thought back. "You just said *Hello.*"

"I'd have written more, but writing without her is like tugging on a leash. Once I figured out you were the Preacher in the story, I began to think. You'd been here, in this room. That might be how we made a connection."

He picked up the remote and turned off the TV. They were back in Room 104. The frail frame of the author was back on the bed, sweating with the bed's top sheet wrapped around his naked body, lips vaguely moving. She was invisible again, and his voice had returned to inside her head.

Maybe if you were close to me spatially, overlapping, it would be stronger.

"But are we really in the same room?" asked Felice, then added, "That wasn't supposed to be as metaphysical as it sounded."

Look out the window, you tell me.

Felice couldn't open the blinds, but she could see through a sliver between them. Outside was the parking lot, the manager's office, and nondescript sign of her motel—though this one's vending machines and restaurant were intact. Signs in the restaurant window offered all-you-can-eat pancakes as well as 'the best damn coffee in the state.' Several cars sat in the lot. A car drove past on the road, followed by an 18-wheeler going the other direction.

But far in the distance, where the city of Fort Rock should have been, was a massive rock outcrop that looked like an anthill—if the ants were the size of tanks.

"What's that?"

Fort Rock. A natural volcanic formation. She liked the name.

Of course, Fort Rock didn't have to be real, but somehow seeing it not there was more unsettling than she expected. She looked back to the parking lot. Across the street, where, in her world, her car had stalled, was an Oregon State Police cruiser. A female officer leaned against the hood, her back to Felice. Felice felt a wave of anxiety hit. What did this mean?

The spell was broken when the woman's partner jogged across the road and handed her a cup of coffee. The woman turned her head. She looked nothing like Felice. Maybe the sign in the window about the coffee wasn't lying; it looked like they performed this ritual here every day.

Felice heard a sigh that turned to a rattle. She looked back at the writer, afraid he would drop dead in front of her. His eyes weren't those of someone who had given up, though, but someone who was haunted with memories he didn't want to relive.

Do you know how writers sometimes talk about their characters as if they're real?

Felice nodded. "Charles Dickens called himself the most wretched man alive when Little Nell died in The Old Curiosity Shop."

I wonder how a better writer like Dickens would handle her. Maybe he could stop her, or control her. Perhaps he'd have gone mad with grief at what he'd be forced to do. Many writers claim to feel their characters as living people, that they sometimes take over the story and do their own things, or whisper 'That's not something I would do' when the writer goes astray.

Felice knew this was true, though she had no idea how. Just like the Dickens and Gulliver references, she didn't remember reading it or seeing it on TV. She just knew.

It's a romantic thought. It's not so much true as it feels true. When you develop a character enough, there are things you know they will and will not do. Just like real people. But this...this is different. Do you know what the Moaners really are?

"Lame George Romero rejects?" Felice bit her lip. "Sorry, I don't mean to keep saying things like that."

The author cracked a smile. *It's okay. That's what I thought, too. But they're not zombies. They're harvesters, and what they harvest is everyone else.* He took a shallow breath and lay down on his side. *Mel is a parasite. She feeds off me, takes my energy. But she doesn't take it directly. She cultivates it, refines it, lets it grow. Then she reaps.*

"And the Moaners are her scythe."

Yes. The words in the book are just the bleached bones that remain once she devours a carcass. The author slowly pointed to his head with a finger gun. *But up here, the people in the stories are real, even the bit players.*

"Like me."

Maybe you started that way, but you're something else now. You fought and clawed your way for every ounce of being and understanding when no one else did. You forced yourself into a narrative that didn't want you and made yourself important to it, to the point where this story can't end without you coming back one more time.

"I don't like the sound of that at all."

I'm sorry, but you know it's true. One way or another, you're going to be there at the end. I'm trying to prepare you for that.

"Are you going to upload kung-fu into my head? Because I could really use that."

The author smiled. *Know your enemy—know yourself.*

Day 7

Felice woke up.

"That's it?" She looked around the room angrily and, unable to find the author, kicked at the part of the bed where he'd sat. "Thanks—a lot—you—jerk! Know your enemy, know yourself. What good is Sun Tzu going to do me now, *and why do I know that's Sun Tzu?*"

She recognized it as a line from a larger passage: *If you know your enemy and know yourself, you will win a hundred battles. If you know yourself but not your enemy you will win one and lose one. If you don't know your enemy or yourself you will lose every time.*

The last thing Felice wanted was fortune cookie military tactics. But that was the way the game had to be played. Fine. Knowing herself seemed like a bit of a problem, but when you took into account a back-story for her hadn't been written in, she actually *did* know everything there was to know. There. Done and dusted. Moving on.

Knowing her enemy. Okay, what did she know about Mel? She was some malevolent imp that got into your brain and humped it until it was too pooped to pop. Too pooped to get up again, ever. Next!

Only that wasn't it and she knew it. She felt she *should* know the answer, but when she got close, something clouded it over. Even the author hadn't said what Mel was, unless she was literally a mad god, in which case everyone was screwed anyway. Mortals couldn't hurt gods, not without a special weapon or a gift from some other god. Pretty much every mythology agreed on that.

Dawn had broken, flooding the motel room with light. She got up off the bed and checked the Gideon. The first chapter of the Book of Revelation was being overwritten. She put the book down and began to pack.

The writer was right about one thing. One way or another, she was going to be there at the end.

Felice was more at peace with her situation than she had any right to be. Strange as it was, the world made sense now—for a given value of sense.

As she rode to the city on a pink bicycle that was too small for her, she didn't feel silly at all. Well, perhaps a little, but in her mind she was riding a Harley, a cigar ground between her teeth, heading toward the final showdown.

"Vroom! Rrrrrrr...RRRRrrrrr....*Screeeee!*" She was only half-aware of the noises she made. She tried not to picture Fort Rock as it was in the writer's world, a large curtain wall of volcanic rock jutting out of the ground like a massive African anthill. It didn't work that way. These worlds intersected, but didn't overlap. She veered around the car pile-up and drove straight for the hermit's lair. She needed to gear up.

Once inside, she checked the event horizon of her new Gideon to see what the others were doing. Groves had three working buses now; the evacuation was ready, but even packed to capacity, that left a hundred people behind. No one felt like drawing straws.

The problem was there simply weren't any more buses. It seemed Fort Rock never had much of a transit system, and most vehicles had been rendered inoperable during the initial panic. Groves didn't know what to tell them, but Felice knew exactly where this was going. She could have predicted the exact moment Agent Groves would feel a tug on the sleeve of his jacket and what the little boy named Mikey would say.

It felt so insidious, looking back. Mikey had been thrilled to remember something from his past, not realizing the *only* reason he remembered was for this very moment, where he would play his part and tell Groves about the bookmobile.

And since he had no other memories she was aware of, his usefulness in that regard was at an end.

She stared at the words *Agent Groves* in the book. "Remember your promise," she said, as if telepathy was only a question of will-power. She knew where they were going. Naturally, Groves wouldn't know where the library was, or the bookmobile, but Mikey would. She had to get there first.

She took a large shotgun off the display rack. An automatic combat model, bigger and badder than her police issue pump action. It didn't just say 'get off my lawn,' it said, 'you gonna fuckin *die*.' She grabbed a bandolier for twelve-gauge slugs, in case she needed to hammer the point home.

Felice stopped short of the piles of clothes that had been the hermit. She looked back at the counter, picked up *The Rise and Fall of the Roman Empire* and laid it on top.

"Thanks."

⚜

The library wasn't far from the bowling alley. As she neared, a knot formed in her stomach. All she found was a burnt out shell. The building had been gutted by fire, probably on Day 1. She stared at the desolate ruins; anger and frustration welled up inside her. What now? What was the point of coming out here?

As if answering, an empty moan came from behind her, then another...and another.

Three Moaners approached her from the bowling alley, roused from whatever hibernation they'd been in when she passed. Two of them might have once been Groves's men. Felice's eyes narrowed. Today was shaping up to be a bad day, and for them it was about to get a whole lot worse.

She took three long steps forward, raised the massive shotgun to her shoulder, and fired. BAM BAM BAM. The Moaners exploded and dropped in dusty heaps.

Felice nodded her approval. "Damn straight." She'd barely felt a kick from the weapon. But she still had no idea what to do next. Then she caught a glint of light reflected off a window. Not from the library, but just behind it.

Of course, the bookmobile wouldn't be *in* the library. Next to the parking lot was a large garage, shared with the local fire department. The doors were shut. She peered in a window. The first two berths were empty, but there on the far end, forgotten and neglected, was the bookmobile. It was painted green and made to look as much like the Very Hungry Caterpillar as possible, right down to the front windshield doubling for its large cartoon insect eyes.

Felice's gut told her the library had burned for a reason other than general chaos. It had Mel written all over it. She was the death of story. Sort of. Eventually. But maybe Mel had an idea about what was going on. Maybe that was why she targeted the woman leading the survivors. Maybe she'd singled out Yuri and the hermit for the same reason. Maybe she knew books were dangerous.

Yet the bookmobile had survived. Why? How? She thought about when Mikey had this glimpse of memory in Haven. It had been after she'd first written in the notebook.

The bookmobile hadn't been here before. It was a recent addition, slipped in by the author. That made it important.

Where were the others now? Felice consulted the Gideon. Groves, the Doc and DJ had almost finished mounting something onto their SUV, but they hadn't left yet. That meant she had time.

Felice worked under the assumption she was under Mel's radar while on her own. So far, that seemed to be holding true. She hadn't seen any more roaming Moaners. Either they were all dead, or being saved for a final battle. Maybe Mel could conjure them as needed. Who knew?

She checked the door next to the garage. Unlocked. Not willing to risk a surprise Moaner meant for Agent Groves, lying in wait to be dispatched with action hero flourish, she poked the door open with her gun and waited. Nothing. Enough light came through the garage windows to see okay, but Felice kept her eyes and ears open, just in case. She padded through the dusty light in her moccasins. The bookmobile lurked at the far end like a cabbage farm's worst nightmare.

It would be unlocked, of course, and Felice would go inside. But what was she looking for? Answers the writer had slipped in through the backdoor. But there would be hundreds of books inside; how would she know what to look for? She had to trust he'd find a way to let her know. An open book on the floor, perhaps. Or a single book sticking out from the shelves, maybe the spines would be arranged in a particular order to hide a secret message.

She needn't have worried. Felice stepped inside and saw row upon row of books, filling shelves all the way down to the back. Enough light came through the windshield to see that although they were of all shapes and sizes, they had the same baby blue and white covers—or at least they would until someone like Groves stepped inside. Felice picked one up and read the title.

Muses.

Felice was so struck by this phenomenon she didn't read any of the books at first. Instead she picked two copies that were vastly different in shape and size and compared them. Fonts, illustrations, columns, everything had been re-sized to fit. It was actually an economical use of mind-space. When you got right down to it, there was only one book on the bus.

She shook herself out of it. This wasn't the time for childlike fascination. The book was here for a reason. As she read, she felt like she wasn't so much learning something new as having the fog lift from her head. Mel did what she could to keep her nature obscured. The writer had never been able to come right out and say her real name or admit what she was. Perhaps he was afraid it would summon her. But even now as she read, Felice felt as if she should have known all along. Wasn't it Plato who said we learn by remembering what we already knew from previous lives?

Of course, Plato was full of shit, too.

Everyone knew a muse was a source of knowledge and inspiration. Artists talked about them all the time, especially to good looking women they wanted to get into bed.

Who and what they were depended on who you asked, and when. To some they were goddesses, water nymphs, or spirits; to others, they were personified abstract concepts. Some said there were three muses, others four. Most of the time the accepted number was nine, covering everything from History and Astronomy to Music and Dance. They were either the daughters of Zeus and Mnemosyne, Uranus and Gaia, or they just popped from springs in the Helicon on their own.

It was all true and none of it was true. They were the stories men made to explain something they knew was real, but couldn't understand. Like Zeus and lightning.

So what was this telling her? She turned the page and stared straight into the drooping empty eyes of a Moaner. Only it wasn't a Moaner, but a mask being held by a woman in a revealing Roman dress and high boots.

Melpomene—Muse of Tragedy.

Know your enemy.

"Well that explains a lot." Felice didn't know what good this would do her. She knew the name of the thing that wanted to kill everyone, so what? If Mel was a goddess, they were all doomed, right? How do you hurt a god, even a minor one?

There was a thump outside.

The thump could have been anything. Anything at all. In no way did it have to be Mel landing just outside the garage door like some kind of super-villain, arriving because the bit player had seen too much.

So why were the hairs on Felice's arms trying to pluck themselves out and make a run for it?

Felice jumped to the driver's seat, laid the shotgun next to her, and tried the ignition. She hoped being inside a reinforced building had protected the vehicle from whatever knocked out the city's power. She couldn't be sure, but while Mel seemed to be in control, it was still the author's world, and he'd said himself science was never his strong point.

The engine turned over, just as someone who didn't at all have to be Mel began wedging her slim fingers under the door and force the garage open. But of course it was her. Felice had summoned her, even if she hadn't said the words. The wide metal door creaked, buckled, bent, and shot open.

Mel was dressed skankier than ever, if that was possible, and looked no older than eighteen. Felice's lip curled. She hit the gas and drove right into her.

She half-expected the bus to stop dead in its tracks as the muse dug her high boot heels into the ground, but barely heard the *thap* of Mel's body hitting the grill. Before she was halfway across the lot, Mel had pulled herself up to the windshields and stared right at Felice.

It wasn't enough to point out the smirk on her face, the kind you wanted to smack off with sandpaper. Nor did the evil gleam in her eye over the scar on her cheek quite get the expression across. You had to look at the condescending face as a whole. Mel was *amused*, and that just pissed Felice off.

Felice slammed the accelerator and headed straight for the building across the street. Maybe the impact wouldn't kill Mel, but it might pin her long enough to figure out what to do next.

To her surprise, Mel jumped off. The smirk had vanished. Had there been a flicker of panic on her face? Felice slammed on the breaks. The bus stopped just short of the wall. Good thing, too. She hadn't put on her seat belt. She grabbed her shotgun and got out.

"Why am I here again?" she asked herself. She had been so full of confidence and bravado ten minutes ago when she gunned down those Moaners, ignoring the fact she'd seen Mel take a hundred bullets, only to wipe them off like so many spitballs fired from straws.

Yet Mel had jumped. She had been afraid. Of what? Messing her hair? Felice didn't see the muse anywhere on the ground or in the sky.

A voice bounced off the walls of the low buildings, coming from everywhere and nowhere. "Go home, Trooper."

Felice's eyes widened. What had she called her?

Mel seemed to read her mind. "Oh, I remember you," she said. "If I wanted you dead, you'd never have survived my escape."

Felice looked to the rooftops. It seemed like Mel's style to look down on people.

"I don't need you," Mel continued, "but I need that bus right where it is. Walk away, or I'll kill you. Simple choice."

Felice hid her smile. Mel *was* worried. She had to be. Why else negotiate? A copy of the Muse book had fallen from the bus. She held it up for Mel to see, wherever she was.

"I know what you are, and it's not even in this book!" She threw it at one of the rooftops, watched it spiral and butterfly in the air till it hit the wall and dropped. "These are just the words of baffled men and women trying to put a face to what you did to them." There was new strength in her voice, which seemed to resonate in the city ruins rather than get swallowed up by them.

Felice was assuming a lot at this point, going with her gut, praying she was right. "You're no goddess. You're some kind of mental parasite. Feeding off a host's thoughts and dreams. Take too much and you drive them mad. But you can't be all like that. Muses are revered, not feared. Nobody ever blamed Van Gogh or Kafka on a muse."

"Maybe they should have."

Well *that* was an unpleasant possibility. "So what's your deal? Just greedy?"

She counted on an explanation; since the earliest Greek tragedies, the villains felt compelled to explain their motivations. She wasn't disappointed.

"You don't know what it's like!" Mel's voice still came from all around, but Felice was sure she had jumped onto the building they'd almost crashed into. "Three hundred years since anyone called upon us. Three hundred years of starvation and slow forgetful madness. *Three hundred years* of being reduced to wandering our own memories, returning to settlements dead for so long they'd been reclaimed by the forests, to the caves where it all began."

Mel appeared on the rooftop, looking down at Felice. Felice kept the gun trained on her, though at this range, even if it could hurt her, it was probably no good.

"There was a time when we were called upon for a simple painting of a horse on a rock face. We helped them shape worlds that never existed, but because of us, were just as real. We helped them win the hearts of those they loved, remember days long gone, plot the stars in the sky, create the very gods they worshiped.

"Three hundred years we'd waited, and when someone finally sought us out as a *joke*, he kept—me—OUT!" The ground shook with a slight tremor. There was more than just anger in her words, there was pain as well.

"So ask me if I care," said Mel. "There's more where he came from." Aside from her looks, the muse reminded Felice more and more of the witch from Hansel and Gretel—there were always more kids willing to eat a gingerbread house.

Felice kept hearing the same words. *Us. We.* "What about the others? They weren't invited to your private buffet?"

Mel laughed. "They've scampered around since the beginning, until I could find them. They'd forgotten themselves and tried to blend in. Not I. I *never* forgot who I was. I've lived the pain and loss I filled into others work, until they were the only things left I could be sure of. While my sisters were surviving as bit characters, I dominated and grew stronger, story by story." The muse chuckled. "And to think, I used to be content with song and dance. I *own* this world, and everything in it. What makes you think you can stop me?"

The fact that you're still talking, for one thing. Felice wondered what was taking Groves and the others so long. Right now it was a standoff, though one she didn't understand. Maybe Mel was waiting for Groves, too. Maybe she didn't want to kill her until Groves and Mikey were there to see it. Melodramatic bitch.

But something Mel had said rattled in her head. The other muses, blending in, surviving...

"Where are they now? The others?"

"They got in the way." Mel didn't elaborate. She didn't need to. Felice remembered the hermit in her bunker, DJ's friend on the rooftop, the woman with the band of survivors. There had been no corpses. Their books—history, astronomy, poetry...

They got in the way? Hardly a reason to hunt them down. They were starting to remember, becoming a threat. *That* seemed more likely. The hermit had written records of the older stories, Yuri helped DJ keep the radio alive, and the Chaucer woman had led a band of survivors to Groves. They seemed to be drawn to the truth like moths to a flame. A flame named Mel, who lived to burn.

Blended in. Bit characters. Forgotten who they were. Felice's heart froze.

"I'm in the way, aren't I?" It wasn't a question. It was a revelation. She remembered the scar on Mel's cheek. Hadn't she shot her there when she fell onto the bus?

The only thing that could hurt a god was another god, or a weapon blessed by them. Mere mortals never stood a chance. They weren't supposed to.

Know your enemy. Know yourself.

She looked up at the roof to taunt Mel, only she wasn't there. Felice spun around, shotgun ready, expecting a collision from any angle. Nothing. She'd blown it. Tipped her hand. Now she really *was* in the way.

Far to the east, the storm clouds had finally broken past the mountains, heading toward Fort Rock. The green flashes of heat lightning were more foreboding than ever.

At first, she thought she heard the rumble of the storm approaching, but she was mistaken. It was a car engine. Groves was coming. The black Escalade pulled into the parking lot, Doc McKay's ridiculous looking ray gun mounted on top. A hole had been cut into the roof so she could stand and operate it. It was smaller than Felice remembered. It was also trained on her.

Groves got out, hand on his sidearm. "Preacher? What the hell are you doing here?"

"Long story."

The FBI man looked her up and down. "How are you feeling?"

"I'm not going to change, but that's not important. Mel is here." Groves scanned the surroundings. "She was on that roof, but she could be anywhere now. Look, there's no time to explain. Get in the bookmobile and go. I'll cover you."

Groves cocked an eyebrow. "You'll...what?"

"I said I'll cover you. Go."

Groves drew his pistol and shot Felice between the eyes. Her head snapped back and she dropped to the ground like a sack of potatoes. He shot her twice more in the chest.

Groves yelled back at the car. "It's a trap! Get the weapon hot!"

"That...fucking...*hurt.*"

Groves turned white as Felice staggered back to her feet. The first bullet had ricocheted off, leaving a large red dot above the bridge of her nose. "Tell me Mikey didn't see you do that." For a second he froze. Long enough for her to grab the gun before he could fire another shot. She slapped him upside the head with her free hand.

"Knock it off, asshole!" Felice didn't remember ever having a migraine before, but figured it had to feel like this. "I told you, I'm not going to change, because I'm *already* like Mel. We're of the same kind, but I'm on your side."

For perhaps the first time, Groves was speechless. His mouth tried to form a rebuttal or at least a half-assed one liner, but couldn't. She couldn't exactly blame him. From his perspective, the story had just gone totally off script, even if he didn't know there was one.

Felice handed the gun back to him and picked up her own. "And tell Doc Holliday there to point her flashlight someplace else."

McKay aimed the contraption away from her. Again, Felice noticed that the gun looked different. "Did you use a shrink ray on your death ray, Doc?"

Doc McKay was quick to pretend this was all normal. "The first machine burnt out. I built a smaller one as a replacement."

Must be great being able to pull imaginary weapons out of your ass like that, Felice thought. The passenger's side of the car opened. Toby got out, but didn't seem to know what to do any more than Groves.

"Where's Mikey?" said Felice.

Toby stammered. "Um, back at Haven. He told us where to find the bus. G-man said he'd be safer there."

Felice glowered at Groves, her teeth clamped shut. "You *what?*" For a split second everything looked much brighter, almost white.

Groves took a step back, trying to calm her down. "I thought Mel would be here. You didn't want me to bring the boy to a hot zone, I hope."

No, but she still wasn't happy about it.

"Um, G-man?" asked Toby. "Are we good? We grabbing the bus or having a gun fight or what?"

Groves seemed to still be waiting to see what Felice would do. Felice shook her head. The only way things were going to move forward was if she forced it. She looked to Toby.

"Were you planning to drive the bus or Mr. Nanny there?" Toby nodded at Groves. "Okay, G-man. You drive. I'll explain." She hopped into the bookmobile. Groves tagged along, still in a daze.

"Why should I trust you?"

"You still have your face, don't you? Come on."

The Escalade led the way back to Haven. They couldn't drive quickly due to the wrecks, stalled cars and building debris the bus had to navigate around. During the trip, Felice fabricated a story that blended the truth with a narrative Groves could handle.

"So there are a number of these gods walking the earth?"

"If you want to call us that, sure." The goddess Felice. She liked the sound of that. A bit intimidating on first dates, though.

"But you...forgot who you were?"

"Something like that."

"And all that cult business with Mel before she was arrested... that was really all about her remembering her true self!"

"Yeah, sure, why not?"

"It all makes sense now!"

"It does? I mean, it *does*."

"So who are you, really?" asked Groves.

"Pardon?"

"Well, if Mel is the spirit of tragedy or whatever, which one are you?"

"I don't know." She hadn't thought about that. Now that he mentioned it, she couldn't get the question out of her head. Of course, if she had to guess—

"Can you fly?" asked Groves. "Break through walls? Heat vision? All the good Superman stuff? I thought I saw your eyes flash white earlier."

"I haven't tried, but I doubt it. She killed most of this city to get as strong as she is."

And God knows how many other worlds.

There was an uncomfortable pause as the two-car convoy worked around a tricky corner filled with rubble from a fallen building.

"Sorry I shot you in the head," said Groves.

Felice laughed. It was a ridiculous thing to say at the best of times.

"I thought you were like Terry, and remember what you told me to do if we met again? Every instinct I had said it was a setup. 'No time to explain?' It sounded like a ruse. My gut's not usually wrong about these things, but it always seems to be wrong about you."

"I'm not exactly in your range of experience."

"You got that right. I don't understand anything anymore. Like why did Mel just leave all of a sudden? She could have crushed us, couldn't she?"

Again, Felice didn't know. Groves was the hero. The rules were different for him.

As they approached Haven, Agent Groves called the base by radio. There was only static.

"I don't like this," he said. Felice agreed. The Cadillac turned down the parking garage ramp, then suddenly stopped while still on an angle. Groves pulled the bookmobile alongside and saw why.

"What happened?" asked Toby over the radio. "Moaners? We were prepared for that!"

Groves shook his head. "Nothing could have prepared us for this."

The barriers were closed, but there was a large hole in the center, as if something had torn through. Both Felice and Groves knew what that meant.

"She's here," they said.

The car wouldn't fit in the hole, and there was no way to open it from the outside. Groves told Doc McKay wait outside and cover the exit with the mini-QROC gun. Toby stayed to protect her while Felice and Groves entered Haven's breached defenses.

Their weapons were out but there seemed little point. The lights were still on, though some had been shot out during the battle. The communications center had been smashed. Brass cases, bullets and guns littered the floor. Three buses, two with armor plates, were lined up facing the exit, ready for a quick escape. They were as empty and lifeless as the rest of the floor. All the signs of a hopeless battle were there, except one thing.

"No bodies," said Groves. He called into his walkie-talkie. "Toby."

"Yeah."

"It's her. Haven's gone."

Felice had a sudden image of Haven as a gingerbread house. All this time everyone here thought they were safe, but really they were just fattening themselves, interacting with Groves, becoming more developed in little ways—until the oven was ready. Mel had waited until Groves left so she could do this away from the main narrative. She couldn't kill Groves, after all. Without him the story ended. She'd save him for the climax. Which was now.

"She's waiting for us," said Felice. "Bottom floor."

"You sense her?"

"I know her."

Doc McKay's voice came over the radio. "David? The storm's getting closer. This is a lost cause. Everyone's dead. We can't stop her. We should just go."

Groves pressed the button on the radio. "Then what? How far do you think we'll get? And we don't know everyone's dead. There could be survivors down there." He looked to Felice to see if he was right. She felt a knot in her stomach as the answer came to her.

"At least one."

Groves took his finger off the radio. "Can we stop her?"

"That's the plan. You just have to trust yourself. You'll take her out."

"Me? *You're* the deity."

Felice shook her head. "I'm not the hero, *you* are. At best I'm Fifth Business. I can't make the kill, but I *can* help get you in a position to. When the time is right, you'll see some dangling electrical wires to jab into her, a grenade to ram down her throat, a spell to chant, I don't know. But it will all work out in the end."

Groves's laughed. "You make it sound like we're in a story."

Felice had forgotten she hadn't broken that news to him yet. "It's more about who we are, the rules we follow because of our nature. Trust me."

Groves's lips tightened. Then he nodded and said into the radio, "We're going in. If we don't contact you in twenty minutes, go." He turned off the radio and put it back on his belt. "Ladies first."

Felice snorted. "Nice."

They descended into the parking garage. The cars making up the second barricade had been pushed aside like toys. Still no bodies, just more guns and brass casings. Felice imagined Mel didn't need to get up close and personal anymore—not the way the Moaners did. She may have just walked through and absorbed everything around her, reaping the final harvest of people that had been slowly getting to know one another, and themselves. So many lives fleshed out just so Mel could take it all.

The real tragedy was how pointless it was. Would anyone remember these stories? The Muses had helped Homer tell the world of the

Siege of Troy. Not the actual Troy, but a Troy that had never existed, yet was nonetheless real. They'd whispered sonnets to Shakespeare about love, showed Galileo the moons of Jupiter, given Bede the Venerable the inside track on English history, and told Leonardo da Vinci what Mona Lisa's smile was *really* all about.

Now one was destroying a man in exchange for a few airport paperback horrors, each more or less the same, just in a different setting. Popular rubbish that sells, but says nothing.

"I am so not cut out for this," said Groves.

Felice was puzzled. "What do you mean? You're FBI. You're trained."

"For *this?*"

"Well, yeah, you have a point there."

They were near the end of the second level, and still no sign of life or death. Groves sighed. "I mean, I sometimes get the feeling I was meant for something else."

"Like what?"

"I dunno. An art historian, maybe, or working the Fraud unit. Does that sound weird?"

"Not as weird as you might think."

The lights on the third floor sub-basement were flickering, probably just for effect. Groves and Felice walked down the ramp together, weapons ready. The floor was clear. No signs of a fight.

When they reached the bottom they saw why they hadn't found any bodies. Every wall here was covered in them.

People Felice had met and talked to, who had given her food and furniture, who had told her about themselves and shared their hopes of escaping the city, all dead. She recognized them by their clothes, but not their faces. Felice looked away, but the pained, sad, empty eyes were all around them, plastered to the wall like some morbid collage.

And there was Mel, sitting on a table in the lab at the back, with her high black boots and night club outfit. Her back was to them.

Groves's voice was a whisper. "It's like the prison."

"What do you mean?"

"We found something like this at the penitentiary when we went to rescue the Doc."

Felice wondered what purpose it served. Perhaps she was just into horror chic interiors.

"Now what?" asked Groves.

"Flank her. I'll get her attention. Wait for an opportunity. Take it. If she sees you, get her to talk. She likes talking."

They approached the lab from opposite sides of the lot, using support pillars to hide their approach. Mel wasn't paying attention. She was talking to someone.

"And what was your doggy's name?"

"Mr. Scruffles."

Mikey's voice. Felice tried not to cry out.

"And what did Mr. Scruffles like to eat?"

"I don't...know."

"*And what did Mr. Scruffles like to eat?*"

"Hot dogs!"

"And where did you like to play with him?"

"Down...by the creek."

"What's your favorite food, Mikey?"

"Chocolate bars," said Felice. Mel's head turned, her smirk meeting the scar on her cheek. Felice had her shotgun trained on the muse, but didn't intend to use it yet. She shrugged. "He hasn't been to a proper restaurant."

"What took you so long?" asked Mel. Mikey stood up, a mix of joy and fear on his face. Before he could say a word, Mel grabbed his shoulder and pulled him close. "That pop gun of yours might sting a bit. Might want to be careful where you point it."

She wanted to say 'let him go,' but that was pointless. "What are you doing with him?"

"Nuts for the winter," Mel replied. "The curtain falls on this dark stage, until it's time to turn the page."

"You're mixing your metaphors. Guess all the power in the world doesn't stop you from being a hack." She willed herself not to look at Agent Groves directly, who was approaching Mel's blindside, making his way to the old QROC gun. No doubt it had one final charge left.

Mel laughed. "Was that supposed to rile me?"

"I want you out, Melpomone."

There was a slight hesitation when Felice used Mel's proper name. The muse narrowed her eyes a moment. "You don't get what you want when I'm around. No one does."

"Find someone else. You're killing the writer."

"Boo fucking hoo."

Groves must have been close enough to hear the comment

about the author. He looked puzzled, but shook it off. He was within range of the QROC gun. The timing felt right. It was now or never.

"If you won't leave willingly," said Felice, "then consider yourself evicted."

Groves hit the button on the QROC gun. It powered up with a hum, and fired. A blue light hit Mel square in the back...

...and she didn't even seem to notice. The QROC had the same effect on her as a flashlight. It sparked and shorted out, the power gauge on its side dropped to zero.

An invisible force slammed into Agent Groves, knocking him into the wall of Moaner bodies. The still forms animated and grabbed him on all sides, pinning his arms, legs and head. Before Groves could say anything, his eyes sank into his head, his mouth and eye sockets pulled down and he became still and gray, part of the horrible bas-relief that enveloped the garage.

Mel had never taken her eyes off Felice. "Evictions require thirty days notice."

Felice's heart had stopped. All her hopes had been pinned on Agent Groves. It only made sense that he would be the one to find Mel's weak spot. He was the hero. Without the hero, the story was over.

Felice was only half-aware she was talking. "He was the hero..."

"I see you're not familiar with my work," said Mel. "In these stories, no one survives. I wait while the world dissolves, until he's ready for the next one. Then I get to play again."

"You call this playing? This city once had twenty thousand people."

Mel rolled her eyes. "And I thought *I* was the melodramatic one. Most of them barely had a thought in their heads. You might as well weep for a colony of insects."

It was hard to accept, but she sensed Mel was right. Most of the population couldn't have been more than an idea of a group, for all she knew copy and pasted like the books in the bookmobile. But there were still plenty of individuals. Haven had been full of them.

"I gave them identity. All of them, no matter how small. A gift from the gods. But contrary to popular belief, we take our gifts back all the time. With interest."

"Santa Claus and Repo Man in one. How efficient." Felice knew this couldn't be true of the others. Mel was, or had become, an aberration. Or maybe she really was just greedy.

The real question was: why hadn't she attacked? What was she waiting for? She had killed the hero without batting an eyelash, had destroyed the other muses one by one, had tried to kill her before—but not now. What was different?

"M-mom?"

Mikey was stiff with fear, held close to Mel's bosom with her arm around his neck. His lip trembled. He had barely gotten out that single word.

Mel smiled. "Isn't that cute? He thinks you're people. When I learned you had been taking care of him, well, I just *had* to hang onto him for a while. Give me something to do while I waited. Watch this. How old are you Mikey?"

"Nine," he answered out of reflex.

"That's something I asked him before. Let's try something new. When is your birthday?"

Mikey's mouth seemed pried open by an unseen hand. "July... thirtieth."

"See that? He resists. That never happens. Not to me. A question is asked, they answer. They think they knew the answer all along. That's how it works. But this boy is different. I wonder why? Perhaps you're a bad influence, Trooper. What else should I ask him? The more he knows the more there is for me to take."

Felice felt like she was walking through a minefield. She had to press onward, knowing each step could be her last. "Just let him go." The words came out sounding as beaten as she felt.

"Why would I do that? I was thinking of keeping him around a while. Ah, who am I kidding? I have no self-control."

"You have me. You don't need him. Let him go."

"Go where? Fort Rock is dead. This world is dead. There is nothing out there for him. The storm has arrived."

The muse must have seen the puzzled look on her face. Fortunately, Mel liked to explain things, and this was no exception. "These stories require the population to be isolated. Trapped within city walls, bridges destroyed, cut off by war or, in this case, a massive electromagnetic pulse. Something to keep everyone trapped together. Makes things easier for me.

"Why do you think this city's electronics no longer worked? The final twist to this story was there had been a nuclear war. Groves knew it, but couldn't bring himself to tell anyone else. The western and eastern seaboards are ash, and the fallout has just arrived. The survivors the writer edits in at the end have only death to look forward to."

"Why?"

"This is the last of the Moaner books. He's of little use to me now. He resists. He hasn't eaten in days, and for once, I can't force him to. I can't play without energy, so I'll wait here and rest until someone with an open mind comes along. A fan, perhaps, coming years later to ask why he hasn't written any more books. Another who seeks advice and inspiration. And I will give it to them. As for the writer? *βάλλ᾽ εἰς κόρακας.*" The ground shook as Mel uttered the words of an ancient tongue.

Felice raised the shotgun, looking down the sights, taking aim at Mel's head. At this range, the spread couldn't be that bad. Mel pulled Mikey directly in front of her so her head rested on his. She slid off the table to stand, bringing the boy with her.

"I wouldn't want you to mess up my looks." She sounded unconcerned, but the scar told a different story. Felice had power, and Mel was afraid of it.

"So what now?" asked Felice. "You hold him there forever? It's me you want, you're just too chicken-shit to fight. If you knew you could take me I'd be dead already. If you knew I could take you, you'd have run away. But you don't want to run; you need to wait for another host. So you're trying to size me up, see if you can take me. See if it's worth the risk."

There was that flicker of concern again. The uncertainty. It's easy to bully when you're omnipotent, but once there's doubt, it's even easier to become a coward.

"I broke free from your grip, gave you that scar. I'm betting none of the others managed to do that."

Mel backed up, step by step, dragging Mikey with her. The boy clutched at her arm trying to get room to breathe, but was helpless in the chokehold. Felice followed, keeping the same distance between them.

Felice reached into her shirt pocket and pulled out her nametag. "T. Felice. I never knew my first name, but right from the start, someone was trying to give me a hint. How much did the others remember before you noticed them? Killed them? Did any of them know who they really were? What you once were? What you had become?"

They passed the broken QROC gun. Mel's back was almost

against the wall of Moaner corpses. She glanced left and right for another way to turn.

"Wh-who are you?" Mel stammered.

"You don't know, do you? Maybe you've forgotten. Who's your counterpart? The ying to your yang? The opposing force of nature?" Felice straightened her shoulders. "I am Thalia, muse of comedy, and this is over."

The fear melted from Mel's face. The smug smirk returned. She tossed Mikey aside and lunged at Felice, something she hadn't expected. Mel jinked before Felice could fire, inhumanly fast, clipping only a bit of her hair. The next thing Felice knew, the muse had lifted her off the ground and hurled her into the wall of Moaners. Their gray bodies grabbed her from all sides, including what was left of Agent Groves.

Mel looked relieved. "I thought you'd *never* get to the point," she said. "I was going to start blubbering next. I mean, geeze, all that dramatic rambling? Kinda treading on my turf there. All that just to find out you're wrong and I was worried for *nothing*? What a waste of time. Comedy? You? That *is* a laugh. I took Thalia back in Görlitzhafen."

Felice blinked. Wrong? How? The wisecracking remarks, the pink bicycle that kept showing up, even the moccasins she wore more or less fit the historical image. History? Astronomy? She already knew who they were. Dance? Singing? She wasn't America's Got Talent material. There were three forms of Poetry, but all she knew were dirty limericks. Who the hell was left?

Mikey had stayed frozen on the ground, helplessly watching the events. Mel pulled him up onto his feet and set him on the table. "You were right, though. With you here I don't need the boy anymore." She wasn't talking about letting him go. "But we should clear a few things up first. Mikey, be a good boy and tell us who your mommy is."

Mikey seemed to be regressing. He no longer made eye contact or spoke, he just pointed in Felice's general direction.

Mel stood close to Felice to catch her every pained expression. "No, she's not your mommy. She's not like you. She doesn't belong here. Who is your mommy?"

Mikey didn't want to answer. His eyes were welling up. Mel brought the boy to Felice so she could see just what was happening. Another identity was being forced inside his head, taking away the person he had made himself, piece by piece.

"Felice!" he said at last.

"No. She's not. Get it through your thick skull. *Who's your mom, brat?*" Mel's voice rumbled like the storm far above them.

Felice could tell the words were there, inside his head, trying to find a way out. Right to the end, he fought her, but it was a hopeless battle.

"Annabelle Mulligan."

Mel smiled, inches away from Felice's. Mikey was gone. Mel would rub salt into this wound until she was bored and then it would be over. Felice's mouth was held shut by a Moaner hand; she couldn't even spit in the bitch's face.

"Annabelle Mulligan," said Mel. "What a nice name. Tell me about her."

Felice looked away. The QROC gun sat on the table in front of her, mocking everything science held dear. Here she was, one of the few surviving people at the end of the world—only she wasn't a person, this wasn't a world, and she wouldn't survive—and part of her still wanted to tell Doc McKay how ludicrous her theories were. Her and her stupid shiny ray gun. Why was it shiny? The world is falling apart around them all, yet she'd taken the time to give it a good polish. Felice could see herself in the flat side of its support base.

"Tell me about your real mom, Mikey."

Again, Mikey resisted, but Felice barely noticed. She couldn't take her eyes off the face staring back at her in the reflection, and where she had seen it before.

She had it all wrong.

Lia had been the first to know. The moment she saw the moaning figures shamble toward her stage, she knew. It was as if she had woken from a dream to find herself in a nightmare.

No one could help. Amidst the panic she'd sought the others. The bard, the lead dancer, the singers, none understood of what she spoke. The Royal Astrologer, who had been in the audience, dismissed her. No one remembered who they were, or understood one of their own had gone mad.

When she had been called to this place to perform, she had brought her sisters. All but one had been welcomed with open arms, and even that one had found her way inside eventually. They had donned new identities to blend in and influence events in their own unique way—to help this land become more than it was.

But it had been such a long time; Lia had forgotten how wonderful it felt to be part of something again, to help create something new. She'd become wrapped up in the beauty of creation, to the point she had almost lost herself within it. The others hadn't fared as well.

Except for one, who no longer wished to serve but to rule.

In the days that followed, as the Duke mounted his futile defense of the keep, Lia sought a way to escape. But there was no way out—her dark sibling had made sure of it.

Too late, she realized her sister had to be stopped before she could do more harm.

Too late, she realized her sister wasn't just hunting people, but her kin, as well.

If only she could wake the others—make them remember—perhaps together they would stand a chance.

Lia could have warned the Duke of the exact moment the inner wall would be breached, but it would do him no good. The force of nature at play here was far too powerful for any army. All she could do was be in the right place at the right time—to delay the inevitable as long as possible.

She headed for the center tower, its guards long gone to defend the perimeter. Perhaps she would buy a few more minutes of life at the top. Her siblings might survive but she would not. She'd made the mistake of catching her sister's eye.

She opened the tower door. At the base of the stairs was a child, a girl three years of age, shivering and afraid. She looked up at Lia with deep blue eyes and screamed.

"Don't let them in!"

Lia shut the door and barred it. "It's okay. They won't get inside." She hated lying to the poor thing, but what else could she do?

The girl rocked back and forth on the step. She was younger than the other children, much younger. There was something familiar about her. Of course, the girl backstage. She'd been rummaging through the prop trunk as if looking for just the right childhood accessories. It felt like a lifetime ago. Lia touched the girl's chin and raised it. "Look at me."

Their gazes locked for a moment before the child pulled away.

It had been long enough. Lia couldn't believe what she'd seen. She put her hand to her chest. "My name is Thalia. You can call me Lia."

"Lia?" the child repeated.

Lia nodded. "Do you remember me?"

The girl sniffled. "I'm sorry I dropped your sword."

Lia was worried the girl might think all this was somehow her own fault.

"It's okay. I didn't mind. Honest. Can you tell me your name?"

"I don't know."

There was no time to be tactful. "*Who are you?*" Lia asked with the full command of her voice.

"*I don't know!*" The tower shook. Perhaps the main gate had been breached. Perhaps. The girl went back to rocking. "I'm scared."

"Of course you are," said Lia. "I'm so sorry. This shouldn't be happening." She wanted to cry, looking at the poor girl. Her whole life should be ahead of her, and instead was going to be cut short. But perhaps there was hope.

There was a thump outside the door.

"I want to go," said the girl.

Lia shook her head. "You can't. Not yet." Lia knew who was on the other side. "I have to give you something first. Look at me." The girl wouldn't. "I can't force you to. Please, look at me." The girl relented. Lia held the child's head with both her hands, looking deep into her eyes.

"Be strong. Hide. Survive. Know where all the moments are. This is my gift to you." Without taking in a breath, Lia blew on the child.

The girl blinked twice. "That's it?"

"That's it."

"Lia?"

"Yes?"

"Your breath stinks."

Lia smiled. "I blame the mutton vendor."

The door cracked and splintered. The girl scampered off the stairs, but didn't scream. She scurried out of sight under the stairwell as a tall figure with fiery red hair walked in.

"Perfect timing," said the woman.

"My thoughts exactly," said Lia, then turned and fled up the stairs.

The girl stayed hidden beneath the stairwell as the red haired woman gave chase. She clutched her knees and cowered. There was a flash the girl could see from the shattered doorway, a sharp cry from the roof, then silence.

She had to go. Now.

The girl ran from the tower. Horrid creatures with masks of pain were everywhere. Some reached out and grabbed at her, but the child managed to avoid them. Around one, through the legs of another, she ducked and weaved and rolled her way to the outermost edge of the city. Most of the creatures weren't interested in her. They seemed to be moving toward the center tower—toward the red haired woman.

She found a small hole in the outer wall as several of the moaning creatures decided to give chase. She barely fit, squeezing through the stone opening just before one could reach her. Its arms clawed at empty air until it gave up and joined the others marching toward the tower. They seemed to be climbing the tower on all sides, surrounding and covering it like a blanket...

She ran. Through forests, streams and hills the girl ran, till she felt she could run no more. There was no thought behind this, only instinct and timing.

The city was dead. Lia was dead. Everyone was dead. Everyone but her.

Exhausted, she collapsed at the top of a wooded hill. For a moment, she thought she saw a man hunched over by a campfire, a strange blue dome next to him. But it was just her imagination. There was no man here, only trees, dead leaves, and darkness.

Shivering, the child covered herself in leaves and slept.

The world faded from memory.

"Tell me about your real mom, Mikey."

Mikey said, "My mom's name is Annabelle Mulligan, but she died in a car crash when I was seven, and her sister took me in and she took care of me even though she works long hours as a police officer and she said as horrible as everything is here one good thing came from it because we got to spend more time together because *she—is—my—mom!"*

Felice pictured the Moaner wall letting her go. It obeyed. Felice pushed past Mel and reached the QROC gun. Mel's eyes bulged, but two Moaners grabbed her arms before she could react. Mikey scrambled off the table and hid underneath.

She wasn't Thalia. The writer had needed a champion who could free him from this enslavement. Someone who truly understood what was at stake, so much so she had taken on the appearance of the woman who inspired him most. But she hadn't been strong enough then. She'd survived by hiding all this time, until she was ready. Until now. There was only one muse she could be.

His.

Felice hit the base of the weapon, which sprang to life and hummed as it powered up.

"Didn't work for him, but you *know* it's going to work for me, don't you?"

Mel cowered. Felice drove her arm through the back of the large solid barrel, which melded with her right up to her elbow. Tiny electric arcs flowed where she and the machine merged. The power gauge on the side shot from empty to full, then cracked.

"Deus Ex Machina. Ain't it a bitch?"

The weapon fired like an old Star Trek phaser, sound effects and all. It enveloped Mel in a cone of blue light, and she screamed as if the skin was being pulled off her body. The attack left Mel dazed and weak. The Moaner arms pulled her back and pinned her to the wall.

Mikey ran up to Felice, who scooped him into a hug.

"That's my boy."

Felice walked over to Mel, holding Mikey in one arm. No wonder she'd had such vitriolic feelings toward her, why even the sight of her was anathema. There was jealousy involved, territoriality, and righteous indignation. The bitch had invaded *her* home and unlike the others, hadn't played nice. That was unforgivable.

Felice had been in all the worlds. She remembered more now. She'd been a child bride in Renaissance France, a teenage heiress in the Victorian era, a refugee during the First World War, and a reporter in downtown Manhattan. She had seen all the worlds fall.

She had been there as the other muses awoke, unprepared for who hunted them, but willing to fight back. She had always been present, though rarely noticed, and in some small way had always tried to help.

She had become strong, hid, survived, because she knew where all the moments were. She'd grown and learned in each of the worlds in ways she was only now beginning to comprehend.

Felice grabbed Mel by the throat and came within an inch of her face. At least the fallen muse had the decency not to beg for her life. You couldn't kill a muse, anyway. Not really. They were ideas, and those never died. But they could be diminished.

"Before I kick your ass out of here, you have something that belongs to me."

"What?"

Felice's eyes sank back into her skull, leaving only two voids. *"Everything."*

The motel manager's wife pushed the laundry cart from room to room, picking up towels and leaving behind fresh bath soap. She paused outside of Room 104, wondering if she should check inside again. The *Do Not Disturb* sign was still there, as always. She had opened the door twice and both times been told to go away. But as long as his credit card held out, her husband was happy to leave the man muttering to himself in the dark.

But what if the writer had a heart attack, or killed himself? The few times she'd seen him at night, he had a haunted look in his eyes, like something out of his stories. She would just check in to make sure he was okay. That's all. And maybe if he had a moment, he could sign his latest book for her and—

The door opened, almost frightening the woman to death. There stood the writer in clothes two sizes too large, sweating, squinting at the daylight. His hair and beard were so ragged it was impossible to recognize him from his book jackets anymore. He shuffled past like a man with an atomic sized hangover, holding one hand over his eyes to block the sun, and headed straight for the diner. He hadn't even noticed the woman.

There was a sign in the window: ALL DAY BREAKFAST— ALL YOU CAN EAT PANCAKES. She watched him walk in, sit down by the window, and point at the sign when the waitress came.

She had a feeling she would have to order a lot more batter.

DAY 1

Felice leaned on the windowsill of her new Chicago apartment, looking down at the busy downtown district. Felice wasn't her name, of course, it was the writer's wife. She had never been aware enough to need a name before. Now that she was, she, well, *liked* it.

The door opened and Mikey came into the living room. "I'm home, Mom!"

Felice smiled. She still loved how that sounded. "How'd it go?"

"Just like you said. They were arguing about chemical aging or something and I was on the street corner selling papers. She thought it was cute, like something out of an old black and white movie. He thought it was child labor and wanted my parents arrested. She bought a paper, the one with the headline where he takes all the credit for the big art bust. She got *mad*."

"Good job, kiddo."

Mike looked at his feet. "I don't think I helped, though. They argued even more."

"Don't worry, that's the way it's supposed to be. It'll work out in the end."

There were still plenty of existential questions she could ask about who she was. About her kind. Where did they come from? Was there someone like her in everyone? How were the Nine different? Was the reason she even existed because they had visited the author? Were the Nine, in a sense, her parents?

But ultimately, what did it matter? She had a purpose. She *was*. That was enough for a person, why not a personification?

Despite all Mel had done, Felice had to thank her. She had learned so much. She had grown. She couldn't fly or break buildings, but she didn't need to. Her job was to help build the world around her and give events a little nudge from time to time. Sometimes to put things on course, sometimes to complicate matters and make them more interesting.

It was never supposed to be about dominating the story, or the characters. Somewhere along the way, Mel had forgotten that. She hadn't only been destroying the author, but the stories as well.

Moaners of the End of Days never saw publication, not like this. The writer's books had gotten progressively more difficult to polish even with the best editors helping, and no amount of editing could fix the fundamental flaws in that mess. In the end, the last of the Moaner books was written by a ghost writer, based loosely off the first half of the novel, before the Preacher character showed up.

The writer took a year off to relax and rethink what he wanted to do. Six months later, after a lot of soul searching, he got back together with his wife. That had made all the difference.

Eventually he fished out the first two chapters of his last book, and remembered he hadn't been trying to write a Moaner story at all, but a romantic comedy about an FBI agent on the trail of art forgers, and the attractive but elitist scientist who was an expert in the field. He wondered if he should give that story another shot.

And when he was ready, Felice had been there waiting for him.

The writer had a friend help him with the science parts.

ABOUT THE AUTHOR

Noah was born in Oshawa, Ontario, and had never quite forgiven it for that. Shortly after university he moved to Tokyo, Japan, where he taught English for three years - yet somehow barely managed to learn a word of Japanese.

After that he moved to London, England to make it as a writer. Unfortunately the closest he came to literary success was working at several bookstores - each of which mysteriously closed down after his stay.

He now lives with his unbelievably patient and supportive wife, Gillian, in Vancouver.

He now wears a hat.

Noah's first novel was Bleeding Heart Yard, a paranormal romantic comedy with werewolves... sorta. In addition, he had a long running comic strip called Fuzzy Knights, which featured the adventures of stuffed toy animals playing Dungeons and Dragons, and the evil hamster trying to destroy them.

The doctors are unsure whether they should increase or decrease his medication.

You can find out more about his peculiarities on his website: http://noahjdchinnbooks.com

CPSIA information can be obtained
at www.ICGtesting.com
Printed in the USA
LVOW12s0614201216
518066LV00001B/4/P

9 781606 593417